A CAT FOR ALL SEASONS . . .

Call 911 M-E-O-W

The police in Tulsa, Oklahoma, received an emergency call from someone so in distress they heard only moans and a high-pitched yowling. Tracing the address, they arrived on the scene, broke through the front door, and found Simba the Siamese desperately gasping for air after becoming entangled in a phone cord. Simba had knocked the receiver off, pushed the preprogrammed button that dialed 9-1-1 . . . and saved his own life!

Vision Sees Daylight

Vision, a three-year-old tricolored tabby, disappeared during her family's move from Maryland to Florida. Upon arriving at their new home, the Williams family put some of their furniture in storage. An incredible forty-two days later, upon checking their belongings, Barbara Williams heard a mewing from a dresser drawer and Vision was rescued . . . weak, dehydrated, but soon fully recovered.

Tricky Trixy

On December 8, 1977, W. A. Bigelow, 79, of Shawnee, Kansas, fell and broke his hip. His feeble cries didn't alert the neighbors, but they brought his small brown Abyssinian, Trixy, on the run. Groaning that he needed help, Bigelow noticed Trixy seemed to listen. Then to his astonishment, she started ringing a nearby dinner bell—unused for years—until neighbors came to investigate. What a hero!

"Please, Mr. Burglar: Bring back our Bootsie!"

In March 1992, burglars broke into an electronics specialty store in Miami and walked right past about half a million dollars in top-of-the-line electronics equipment. The sole object of their felonious quest was Bootsie, a seven-year-old black-and-white back-alley tom cat of mixed breed. All fifteen employees were crestfallen at the catnapping of the store's mascot.

BRAD STEIGER is the author of more than 100 books with over 15 million copies in print, including *Valentino*, *Judy Garland*, *The Healing Power of Love*, *Strangers from the Stars*, and from Signet Books, *Bizarre Crime*. Together with his wife, Sherry Hansen Steiger, he appears frequently on such television and radio shows as *The Joan Rivers Show*, *Entertainment Tonight*, and *Hard Copy*. They live in Forest City, Iowa.

CATS
INCREDIBLE!

True Stories of
Fantastic Feline Feats

BRAD STEIGER

A PLUME BOOK

PLUME
Published by the Penguin Group
Penguin Books USA Inc., 375 Hudson Street,
New York, New York 10014, U.S.A.
Penguin Books Ltd, 27 Wrights Lane, London W8 5TZ, England
Penguin Books Australia Ltd, Ringwood, Victoria, Australia
Penguin Books Canada Ltd, 10 Alcorn Avenue,
Toronto, Ontario, Canada M4V 3B2
Penguin Books (N.Z.) Ltd, 182–190 Wairau Road, Auckland 10, New Zealand

Penguin Books Ltd, Registered Offices: Harmondsworth, Middlesex, England

First published by Plume/Meridian, an imprint of Dutton Signet,
a division of Penguin Books USA Inc.

First Printing, March, 1994
10 9 8 7

REGISTERED TRADEMARK—MARCA REGISTRADA

LIBRARY OF CONGRESS CATALOGING IN PUBLICATION DATA:
Steiger, Brad.
    Cats incredible! : true stories of fantastic feline feats / Brad Steiger.
        p.   cm.
    ISBN 0-452-27159-2
    1. Cats—Miscellanea.   2. Cats—Humor. I. Title.
SF445.5.S74   1994
636.8—dc20

                                                    93-26521   CIP

Printed in the United States of America
Set in Goudy Old Style
Designed by Eve L. Kirch

BOOKS ARE AVAILABLE AT QUANTITY DISCOUNTS WHEN USED TO PROMOTE PRODUCTS OR
SERVICES. FOR INFORMATION PLEASE WRITE TO PREMIUM MARKETING DIVISION, PENGUIN
BOOKS USA INC., 375 HUDSON STREET, NEW YORK, NEW YORK 10014.

CONTENTS

3. KITTY, COME HOME! 37

4. THE TOUGH GUYS—CATS WITH MORE THAN NINE LIVES 61

8. FIND YOUR IDEAL CAT IN THE STARS

1

FANTASTIC FELINE FACTS ABOUT OUR NUMBER ONE PET

Cats seem to be everywhere these days. The Cat Fancier's Association now recognizes thirty-five different breeds of our feline friends. With an estimated 62.4 million of the furry creatures in the United States alone, their number has doubled in the past decade.

Cats are living longer. The average life expectancy of cats has nearly doubled since the 1930s—from eight years to sixteen.

The oldest living cat on record. Although a cat is not really considered a senior citizen until after his or her tenth birthday, the longevity champ is Puss: He passed away in 1939, just one day after the celebration of his thirty-sixth natal anniversary.

Cats are prolific critters. The cat's fertile nature, together with improved health care, has certainly contributed to the animal's current numbers. Mother cats have produced as many as nineteen kittens per litter.

The largest recorded number of kittens born in a lifetime of fertility to a single female cat is 420.

And *we do take good care of them.* In an average year, cat owners in the United States spend $2.15 billion on cat food—and $295 million on cat litter.

Goodbye, *Felix and Josephine.* Today the most popular names for pet cats are Tiger and Samantha.

What *a rough tongue you have, Samantha!* Those sandpaper kisses from your pet are due to numerous tiny knobs called papillae on the surface of Kitty's tongue. They are shaped like backward hooks and are designed to hold food and to provide the abrasiveness your cat needs for those endless hours of grooming.

A *whole lot of sleeping going on.* Yes, your cat does sleep a lot. Cats are, in fact, the sleepiest of all mammals. If you added up all the minutes your pet spends in catnaps, the total would probably hover around sixteen hours.

If, however, for any reason your cat should be deprived of the amino acid tryptophan, which is found in milk, eggs, and poultry, he or she would become a jittery insomniac in very short order.

Your *powers of observation have served you well: Your cat does have more than one eyelid.* As a matter of fact, all cats have three.

C*ats can't really see in the dark.* And their daytime vision is only fair—but they can see better than their owners in semidarkness.

Their eyes don't really shine in the dark, either. Cats' eyes contain highly reflective cells that collect light from even very dim sources. When you flash a light on a cat in the darkness, these reflective cells make it appear that the cat's eyes are glowing.

Although cats have long been thought color-blind, recent tests indicate that they can distinguish between some basic colors, such as red and blue, when the colors are paired.

B*ut, boy, do they have good ears!* A cat's hearing rates as one of the sharpest in all the animal kingdom. If you've ever wondered why your cat is always waiting for you at the door, the explanation is that he or she can hear your footsteps from hundreds of feet away.

T*hose darned mice are singing off-key again!* It has long been noted that cats are supersensitive to discord and will soon vacate a room where out-of-tune singers or musicians are performing. On the other hand, cats appear genuinely to appreciate good music and harmony.

Biologists have studied a number of "singing" mice that exhibit two-octave ranges and tempos varying between two and six notes per second. It is quite likely that all mice sing, producing songs similar to the chirping and twittering of small birds, but with a great deal more variety.

If you have not been aware of any rodent chorales, it is probably because the vast majority of mice sing far too high for the human ear, perhaps much like the supersonic squeaks of bats. The mice you *have* heard may be compared to the basses and baritones of a human choral group; most of their fellow warblers are high sopranos.

While undoubtedly a few humans have the auditory sensitivity to eavesdrop on a night at the rodent opera, it may be assumed that cats, with their remarkable hearing, present a captive audience to the pesty little chirpers. Everyone knows that cats enjoy an occasional snack of mouse meat, but some scientists have theorized that cats primarily pursue mice when the little buggers sing off-key and upset the feline insistence on harmony.

Many famous musicians and composers have partly credited their success to their critical cats' acceptance or rejection of their work. Imagine those unfortunate miniature madrigal singers, the mice, receiving the ultimate negative criticism of their performance from a cat with a splitting headache!

The World's Champion Mouse Catcher. In light of the fantastic feline fact detailed above, Towser, a female tabby in charge of rodent control at a Scottish distillery, was either the world's champion mouse catcher or the world's most sensitive music critic. At any rate, by the age of twenty-one, the records show that Towser had caught 23,000 mice.

Your cat does walk differently from your dog. The giraffe, the camel, and the cat are the only animals with a gait in which front and hind legs move together first on one side, then on the other.

Cats are also the only clawed creatures that walk on their claws rather than their paw pads.

In the northeastern United States, cats are frequently born with six or seven toes on one paw.

Most of the time, cats do land on their feet. Each year, hundreds of cats fall from high tree branches, roofs of houses, and open windows of high-rise apartment buildings—and yet most of them manage to survive relatively unscathed. Although over the centuries monstrous children have tested the hypothesis that cats always land on their feet, serious researchers have recently discovered that cats falling from seven to as many as thirty-two stories have the ability to "parachute" safely to the ground by spreading their legs and arching their backs, thereby distributing the points of impact fairly evenly and lessening the likelihood of serious or fatal injury.

A few years ago, a pregnant cat named Pat was accidentally bumped off a high bridge in Portland, Oregon. Pat not only survived the fall, but she gave birth to a healthy litter of kittens a few days later.

That's not a mustache your cat wears. You should never trim your cat's whiskers, even if they're too long to suit your esthetic criteria. Your cat uses those whiskers to find his or her way in the dark and to determine whether or not he or she can fit into—and out of—a tight place.

Once and for all, cats do not need to be bathed. There's a very good reason why cats naturally avoid water, and your well-intentioned bathing of your cat can actually be harmful. Soaps and detergents may remove natural oils, and if the cat should become chilled during a bath, his or her resistance to infection drops.

Cats are so fastidious by nature that they spend an average of 30 percent of their waking hours grooming themselves with their own moist little tongues.

Correction: Not all cats avoid water. That's right. The Van cat, a breed native to Turkey and rarely seen outside that country, loves to swim.

Scratch my back, and I'll scratch yours. When your cat rubs against your leg, he or she is not only making friendly contact and massaging his or her back against your ankle bone, but is also trading scents with you. That way, you become more catlike, and your pet feels that he or she has become more human.

Your feline friends are not finicky if they take a long time to smell their food. Cats also use their noses as their thermometers. If they take a while to sniff that bowl of warm milk you just served, you probably made it too hot, and they are just waiting for it to cool down to avoid a burned tongue.

Please, no sweets for your feline sweetie! At least not chocolate. You may think chocolate is to die for, but it can be fatal to your cat. For one thing, the popular sweet contains oxalic acid, which prevents calcium absorption; for another, it contains the alkaloid theobromine, which is toxic to cats.

Never give your cat two aspirins and call the veterinarian in the morning. Aspirin is poison to your cat.

Your dog's favorite food can make your cat go blind. Don't try to economize by feeding dog food to both your canine companion and your cat. Dog food lacks taurine, a substance necessary for your feline friend's eyesight and healthy heart.

You say you keep finding cat hair everywhere? Maybe cats are basically nocturnal creatures because they shed more in the light. Your cat companion will lose more hair in the summer, of course. But be advised that electric lights also cause cat hair to fall out—and that includes the illumination from your television set.

Not every cat is warm and friendly. Animal researchers have determined that about 15 percent of all kittens will resist domestication and socialization with human beings. Interestingly, such felines are not the flighty, temperamental ones, but the ones in the litter that appear very slow and quiet.

You listen; I'll talk. Cats have always made good listeners, especially as they sit on your lap being petted. A recent survey discovered that only 5 percent of all cat owners do *not* talk to their feline pets.

The crown for the world's heaviest cat. No tubby tabby has yet bested the record set by Himmy, an Australian cat that tipped the scales at forty-five pounds, ten ounces in 1982.

In 1991, the tabloid *National Enquirer* conducted a contest to determine the heaviest cat among those owned by its millions of readers. The winner was Spike, a thirty-seven-pound, thirteen-and-a-half-ounce tabby owned by Gary Kirkpatrick of Madrid, Iowa.

In 1992, the *National Examiner*'s Fattest Cat in America contest located Morris, a tubby tomcat owned by Fred and Jeannie Scott of Ottawa, Kansas. Morris weighed in at a hefty thirty-six pounds.

The runner-up in the competition was Tiger, a thirty-three-pound brown tabby belonging to Paul and Teri Hammer of Excelsior, Minnesota.

Before we leave considerations of size to go on to another topic, it should be mentioned that the world's smallest breed is the Singapura, a street cat that lives in drains in Singapore.

The world's richest cats. Nicodemus lived a true ugly duckling story. The unwanted runt of a pedigreed litter, Nicky was given to New Yorker Loiselle Adams, and he grew into a glamorous, snowy-white Persian and worked as a famous model for Revlon cosmetics.

In the 1960s, Nicodemus went on to become a cottage industry. The sophisticated cat even appeared on *The Today Show, Captain Kangaroo, Play Your Hunch,* and many other television shows.

When Walt Disney was looking for a cat to costar in the 1963 film *The Incredible Journey,* veteran animal trainer Al Koehler went on a "talent hunt" to the Chafee Humane Association Pound in Ontario, a suburb of Los Angeles. There Koehler bought the Siamese that Disney himself came to name Syn Cat, "because he synchronizes so well with everything."

Koehler declared that Syn Cat was "the smartest, most sociable, most emotionally stable cat in the world." Proclaiming the affable Siamese a cat that comes around only once in a lifetime, Koehler saw Syn Cat go on to star in such other memorable Disney films as *That Darn Cat* (1965) with Hayley Mills and Dean Jones.

In the early 1960s, two fifteen-year-old cats, Hellcat and Brownie, inherited nearly $500,000 from the estate of Dr. William Grier of San Diego.

About the same time, a white alley cat named Charlie Chan inherited the entire estate of his owner, Grace Alma Patterson of Joplin, Missouri. Patterson stipulated in her will that when Charlie died, the three-bedroom house, the seven-acre pet cemetery, and the quarter-million-dollar collection of antiques were to be auctioned off and the proceeds donated to local and national pet charities.

On July 25, 1991, Damon and Pythias, a pair of six-year-old Burmese, inherited the $750,000 Fifth Avenue co-op of millionaire widow Terry Krumholz.

The will required cat caretakers to perform regularly such duties as the administration of hairball medication and the provision of proper toys.

Englishwoman Muriel Fletcher wanted to be certain her beloved Blackie would be well cared for after her death, so she left her cat a fortune of $100,000. When Fletcher passed on in 1991, Blackie was able to take up residence in a plush cattery owned by Don and Mimi Cottrell.

Blackie was already acquainted with the Cottrells; they had cared for him when Fletcher went on her annual vacations. They note that although Blackie could dine on steak and salmon at every meal if he wished, the wealthy cat prefers Little Friskies.

The Cottrells won't be adding to their own bank account when Blackie joins his mistress on the Other Side. Whatever cash remains will be equally divided between the Society for the Prevention of Cruelty to Animals and a local animal welfare society in Great Britain.

Eccentric miser Ben Rea, a British bachelor landlord so frugal that he wore his tenants' cast-off clothing, died in 1990 at the age of eighty-two and left his fortune of $14 million not to one cat, but to three charities that support stray felines.

Not a single one of Rea's furious relatives got a penny from the sale of his ten houses and his collection of elegant antiques. Even his sixty-six-year-old housekeeper, who had looked after the old man for forty years, received nothing for her decades of devotion.

"I'm really not surprised," said Ms. Martin, Ben Rea's housekeeper. "The only thing he cared about was cats. He had only Blackie when he died, but he had owned as many as fifteen cats at a time."

Yet another cat named Blackie strayed onto the property of Dorothy Walker just three years before her death. This Blackie ended up the ward of Britain's Royal Society for the Prevention of Cruelty to Animals, which will receive Walker's bequest of $5 million on the condition that Blackie gets loving treatment until he journeys to cat heaven.

Walker never joined the society or contributed to any animal charity during her lifetime, but she often told her housekeeper she thought more highly of animals than of human beings. Although she expressed the opinion that anyone found guilty of cruelty to animals should receive the death penalty, Walker had never owned a pet until Blackie strayed into her house.

In 1992 Cyrus, a seven-year-old cat, inherited an $850,000 mansion in Bridgeport, Connecticut, that boasts a litter box in every one of its fifty rooms.

Horace Venting, the attorney for Cyrus's late owner, Beatrice Farrington, said his client feared that her beloved Cyrus would be neglected by her surviving relatives, so she clarified matters by leaving her entire estate to the cat.

As we leave our feline friends to enjoy their fabled riches, I close by suggesting that all the stray cats in France may well be purring harmoniously in gratitude for the benevolence of the elderly couple Lucien and Marcelle Bourdon, who recently auctioned off fifty-four valuable paintings and donated a mind-boggling $60 million to charities that look after abandoned cats.

CATS COURAGEOUS

Dr. Frank S. Caprio, a psychologist and author, has noted that cat owners are healthier and happier and live longer than catless individuals. "Talking to your cat," Caprio says, "is one of the best stress-relief valves you can have."

In this chapter we learn that some cat owners are healthier and happier and will live longer because their pet saved their lives.

On Christmas morning, 1990, Jack, a young tiger tabby, awakened single mother Corrie Owens and her five-month-old son, Brandon, with high-pitched mewing and rescued them from a five-alarm fire in an apartment building in Montreal.

In St. Paul, on August 23, 1991, Minnie, a Maltese, kept jumping on her sleeping mistress's chest until she awakened. The cat knew something in the air just didn't smell right. Rose Daigle managed to get out of her gas-filled room before she fell into the ultimate sleep.

In Modesto, California, in the fall of 1990, a cat called Oscar saved four-month-old Anthony Phillips from choking to death in his crib by creating a fuss in the infant's bedroom and drawing his mother, Kandy, to investigate the disturbance.

Trixy Rings the Bell and Brings Help for Her Injured Owner

On December 8, 1977, a small brown Abyssinian named Trixy was responsible for bringing aid to her injured owner, seventy-nine-year-old W. A. Bigelow of Shawnee, Kansas.

Bigelow had fallen on the concrete walkway in front of his home and had broken his hip. Unable to move, the elderly man lay helpless in his pain. His feeble cries for help failed to reach his neighbors.

Then Trixy, his cat, bounded into view.

Cocking her head quizzically from side to side, Trixy seemed to be thinking the situation through carefully.

"I need . . . help. I can't . . . get up," Bigelow managed to say. Then, even in his pain, a wry chuckle escaped him as he reminded himself that he was talking to a cat. What did he expect Trixy to do? Carry him into the house and call an ambulance?

Trixy began to pace nervously around her fallen owner. Suddenly her attention seemed to be directed to a dinner bell that hung outside the house, a remnant of a happier time in Bigelow's life—a time when his wife was alive and their children were still at home.

The dinner bell! Bigelow groaned inwardly. He had only re-cently tied the rope up so that Trixy couldn't playfully tug at it and annoy his neighbors by ringing the bell.

Trixy had not attempted to ring the bell since her master had scolded her and fastened the rope up out of her reach. But now she leaped a good three feet in the air and managed to snare the rope with her teeth, bringing forth a resounding clang.

The little Abyssinian kept her jaws stubbornly clamped around the rope and swung her weight from side to side, vigor-ously ringing the bell. Twice Trixy lost her hold on the rope and had to make a new jump—but she triumphantly rang the bell again and again.

It almost seemed as if Trixy were proud of herself when the first of the neighbors came running to see what was wrong and found her owner lying on the walkway.

In hardly any time, someone had called an ambulance and Bigelow was on his way to the hospital. While he recuperated there, his son and daughter-in-law cared for Trixy in a manner that befitted a true hero.

A Sluggish Twenty-Pound Tabby Proves More than a Match for a German Shepherd That Attacks a Five-Year-Old-Boy

Five-year-old Jimmy Pickett of Boise, Idaho, was on the brink of driving his mother, Melinda, insane. Early that September morning in 1989 the weather had been cold and rainy, and Jimmy had to stay inside to watch television and color in his *Little Mermaid* coloring book. Now that the sun was out and drying up the puddles, the two-legged perpetual motion machine wanted to go outside and play on the tire swing his father had hung from the low branch of the maple tree in the backyard.

"Can Godzilla come with me?" Jimmy asked, referring to the four-year-old red tabby that had grown from a sickly, undersized kitten to a hefty twenty-pounder. Godzilla had originally been christened Sammy, but when he just kept growing and growing, Melinda's husband, Jack, had come up with an appropriate nickname.

"Try and keep Godzilla inside the house when you go out to play," Melinda said, laughing. The big cat loved to be with Jimmy, but had become so sluggish and lazy that he would probably just curl up near the maple tree and take a nap in the sun.

"Now, remember," Melinda called after her son as he bolted through the screen door, "don't either you or Godzilla tease Geronimo!"

The Lober family next door had a fourteen-year-old German shepherd named Geronimo that had recently turned mean. The very sight of Godzilla sent the dog into a frenzy, and sometimes Jimmy's shouts and laughter apparently got on his nerves.

Godzilla the cat had a mischievous streak: In spite of his bulk, he would strut back and forth on the top rail of the old wooden fence, teasing Geronimo and staying just out of the shepherd's jumping range. Melinda worried that the fence was getting rickety. If the big shepherd ever got upset enough, he might break the rails to get at Godzilla or Jimmy.

Melinda became so involved in her favorite soap opera that afternoon that she heard nothing unusual until Jimmy's screams jolted her back from the world of television fantasy.

Angry growls told her that her son's screams meant something much more terrible than a tumble off the tire swing.

As she ran out the back door, she was horrified to see that Geronimo had Jimmy down on the ground. Melinda herself screamed as the German shepherd, which weighed at least 120 pounds, clamped his jaws around Jimmy's left arm and began shaking the boy as if he were a rat.

That was when fat, sluggish Godzilla, normally the gentlest of cats, leaped from the tree onto Geronimo's back. Godzilla's furious growls replaced the dog's snarls.

Before Melinda could confront the vicious shepherd, he had released Jimmy with a yelp of pain. Godzilla had sunk his claws into Geronimo's back. The dog beat a hasty retreat into his own yard, Godzilla still clinging to him.

Jimmy had been severely bitten; Melinda saw gaping wounds dangerously near his eyes and jugular vein. As she scooped up her son in her trembling arms, she knew he would require many stitches and hospital care—but thank God and Godzilla, none of the wounds appeared to be life-threatening.

"We know that Godzilla saved Jimmy's life," Melinda said. "If Geronimo had mangled him for only a few more seconds, his huge teeth might have torn a fatal wound in his throat. The police came to get the German shepherd and to dispose of him—something the Lobers should have done as soon as he started getting mean.

"When Jack and I got back from the hospital that day, we gave Godzilla a large plate of liver," she said. "We decided that we didn't care if he grew to weigh fifty pounds. We knew that he would always come to our rescue no matter how fat he got."

Bartholomew's "Nose-Punching" Saves a Family from Fire

In October 1991, twenty-six-year-old Lucille Melander, who lived in a suburb of Little Rock, Arkansas, was taking a nap in her bedroom when Bartholomew, her nine-year-old Russian Blue, began to strike at her nose with his paw.

"I was startled and kind of angry," Melander said. "I'd had Bartholomew since I was seventeen, and he had never taken such liberties with me."

As she sat up to chase the cat off her bed, Melander woke up enough to smell the smoke that was issuing into her bedroom.

"I jumped out of bed and looked out into the front rooms," she said. "There was a raging fire in the living room, and I saw that the best thing to do was to grab the kids and get out of there fast. My husband, Danny, had already left for work, so I knew I had to do it myself."

As thick, acrid clouds of smoke began to swirl around her, Melander ran into the nursery and quickly grabbed her eighteen-month-old twin girls from their beds.

"Bartholomew was right at my side," she said. "It was as if he had to be certain I knew what to do in such an emergency. It was actually a good thing that he stayed with me, because the smoke was getting thicker and thicker, and once when I started to run in the wrong direction, he bit me in the ankle and directed me to safety."

Lucille Melander and her husband lost their new suburban

home, but she was able to save the lives of their daughters, as well as her own life—and that of Bartholomew.

"Bartholomew was the one who saved our lives," she said. "If he hadn't started to use my nose for a punching bag, I might well have stayed asleep until it was too late to save the girls—or myself.

"I had always felt that we had developed a strong telepathic rapport during our nine years together," Melander concluded. "Bartholomew certainly proved his love for me and for my daughters by helping to get us out of that burning house."

Mary Poppins Rescues a Two-Year-Old from a Rattlesnake

In July 1990, Varee Reeves, of Mesa, Arizona, was about to join her two-year-old, Gene, in their backyard when she heard what she at first thought was the sound of a broken sprinkler.

"We had recently installed an automatic sprinkler system to water the various plants in our yard," Reeves said. "We had had a little trouble with the pipes bursting as we installed the system under the sand, so I thought, 'Oh, no, here we go again—water is spraying out from a leak.'"

But as she listened more closely, she realized she was not hearing the hiss of escaping water, but the angry hissing of their new cat, a white Turkish Angora named Mary Poppins.

"Thinking Gene might be teasing Mary Poppins and be cruising for a good scratching," Reeves said, "I picked up my sunglasses and the romance novel I was reading and pushed open the sliding glass door that led to the backyard.

"I think my heart literally stopped beating when I saw a rattlesnake moving slowly toward Gene. The only thing that blocked the snake's path was Mary Poppins, who was bobbing and weaving in front of it."

Reeves grabbed the outside telephone and quickly punched 911. Somehow she managed to describe the horror that was unfolding in the backyard—and to tell the officers to hurry.

The snake was now coiled, and its rattles were buzzing. But Mary Poppins refused to back down. She sat up on her haunches and met the snake's hypnotic stare with a withering glare of her own.

"It was truly as if Mary Poppins were a snake charmer, weaving her supple white body back and forth before the fierce and deadly triangular head of the rattlesnake," Varee Reeves wrote to me. "She seemed deliberately to be causing the snake to focus its attention on her swaying white body and to distract it from its deadly movement toward Gene. My two-year-old son simply sat there, completely transfixed by the incredible action drama taking place before his widened eyes."

Then a most remarkable thing occurred. The rattlesnake relaxed its coiled position and began to retreat slowly, edging away from the cat.

"I saw that the thing was over four feet long, and I became even more frightened than ever," Reeves said. "But it also flashed in my mind to wonder if somehow during their staring contest Mary Poppins had telepathically sent a frightening message to the snake that had made it retreat."

Several times the snake appeared to rally and begin another try at the boy.

"Mary Poppins would be right there, standing her ground, staring at the invader with her unblinking blue eyes," Reeves said, "and the snake would once again be forced to retreat."

Within minutes two police officers and a man from the

reptile control bureau arrived. While the policemen stood guard, the reptile handler deftly caught the rattlesnake with a looped pole and dropped it writhing into a canvas sack.

"We'll take Mr. Rattlesnake back out to the desert where he belongs," an officer told Gene.

"Okay. Good," the two-year-old finally said, nodding vigorously, at last breaking the spell under which he seemed to have been held.

Gene's mother said Mary Poppins was rewarded with a can of top-grade cat food. "We're thinking of renaming her, though. Maybe 'Wonder Woman' is a better name for her after she saved Gene from the rattlesnake."

Eighty-Year-Old Russian's Cat Keeps Him Alive

In the summer of 1992, the Associated Press carried an item which quoted the *Komsomolets Kubani* newspaper's account about an eighty-year-old man who was being kept alive solely by the benevolent actions of his cat.

According to the story—also transmitted by the NEGA news agency—the man's feline benefactor caught pigeons and brought them home to his hungry master, who made pigeon noodle soup with the day's catch.

Realizing that he had an enviable solution to the economic hardships plaguing the nation, the elderly man sought to have his cat insured with the state insurance authorities in his southern Russian town of Labinsk. The cat was, after all, his sole means of support. To his dismay, the unsympathetic insurance officials turned down his petition.

The newspaper report went on to say that the man had taken his complaint to President Boris Yeltsin, arguing that elderly people on fixed incomes were the ones hardest hit by economic reforms.

Without the keen hunting prowess of his generous cat, the eighty-year-old man pleaded his case, he would surely starve to death.

Sinbad the Siamese and the Halloween Mirror

"What is wrong with Sinbad?" Clark Henricksen asked his friend Susan Davidowicz. "Your normally gregarious Siamese has been doing nothing for the past hour but sitting on the sofa and staring up at the plate-glass mirror in the dining room."

Davidowicz had no immediate explanation. Sinbad had been in Henricksen's apartment on several previous occasions. Henricksen had asked her to help him decorate for a Halloween party that October night in 1992, and she had brought Sinbad along with her.

"Since there will only be eight of us, I want to have a sit-down dinner around the table," Henricksen said, quickly diverted from the mystery of Sinbad's obsession with the large mirror. "I'll light a fire, and we can sit around telling ghost stories after we eat. The reflection of the flames in the big mirror ought to really heighten the eerie effect."

Davidowicz laughed. "Maybe there is already a ghost here. I mean, the way Sinbad keeps staring at the mirror over the dining room table. Isn't there some old legend about a cat looking into a mirror on Halloween?"

Henricksen opened a box of orange and black streamers for the ceiling. "I believe you're thinking of a sweetheart looking into a mirror on Valentine's Day and seeing an image of her future mate," he said.

Davidowicz shrugged. "Maybe. But isn't there another old legend about looking into a mirror and seeing ghosts standing behind you?"

Henricksen sighed as he handed her a roll of tape and several of the crepe-paper streamers. "Maybe you saw that in *Freddy Krueger Meets Frankenstein and the Wolfman on Elm Street*," he teased her.

Davidowicz laughed but then knelt on the sofa beside her pet. "What is it, Sinbad? You know something about that mirror, don't you? Come on, old buddy. You know you can tell me. What is the deep, dark secret of the mirror above Clark's dining room table?"

She was about to put her ear next to Sinbad's mouth, pretending to listen for a whispered revelation, when the Siamese emitted such a loud, pitiful wail that she nearly fell off the sofa. She recovered just in time to see the heavy mirror pulling away from the dining room wall.

"Clark! Help!" she shouted as she managed to catch the mirror in midair and steady it against the back of the sofa. Within seconds Henricksen was at her side to take most of the mirror's hundred-pound weight.

After several telephone calls, Henricksen remembered a repairman who owed him a favor and who agreed to come to the apartment to fix the mirror before the Halloween party started. The repairman said the mirror probably had been loose for months and could have come crashing down at any time.

"Good Lord, Susan," Henricksen exclaimed after the repairman had finished the work and left the apartment. "Don't you just hate to think what could have happened if that mirror had shattered on us as we sat around the dinner table tonight!"

Davidowicz nodded quietly, then added, "Thank heavens for Sinbad. It's obvious that he managed somehow to tune in to the loose mirror, and he just sat there staring at it, trying to warn us."

"He did a good job of it," Henricksen agreed. "Especially that wail, like a tormented Halloween spirit from Hell."

Davidowicz smiled. "And now we truly have a Halloween legend to tell people about Siamese cats and mirrors."

Snowball Saves a Baby from Death by Strangulation

Paula had acquired Snowball, a white Persian, four years before marrying Stanley Wiggs. Fortunately, Wiggs liked cats, and the three of them moved into a new apartment in Akron in 1989.

"I was a little concerned when the baby came along a couple of years later," Paula Wiggs admitted. "By then I had had Snowball for nearly seven years. I was afraid he might be jealous and do something to hurt our son, Keith. I mean, you hear all those old wives' tales about cats sucking the breath out of babies."

But Snowball remained a loyal companion to his mistress, and his only response to the infant seemed to be the expected catlike curiosity.

When Keith was about nine months old, Snowball proved that he could be more than a faithful pet—he could also be a lifesaver.

Paula was in the kitchen chopping vegetables for beef stew, one of Stan's favorite dinners. "Snowball started howling at the top of his lungs, which really startled me, because normally he is a very quiet cat. The only time that he ever yowled or fussed was if his litter box somehow got pushed in the kitchen closet and the door got accidentally closed."

Paula thought the irritating howling would soon cease, but Snowball continued his unappreciated solo.

"What do you want?" Paula shouted, expecting him to come running at her call. In a moment Snowball's big white head would peek around the corner, the yowling would stop and the mystery would be solved.

Snowball did not appear, but Paula went on chopping vegetables for the stew, intent on fixing dinner, trying her best to ignore Snowball's caterwauling.

"Be quiet, you monster!" she yelled at her noisy pet when his screams grew even more intense.

In retrospect, Paula said, she should have realized at once that something was wrong. "Snowball was usually so quiet. Such unrestrained screeching was definitely not his style. It was just that I was so damned intent on making that beef stew taste like the kind Mom used to make."

Finally Snowball's cries reached a pitch that could no longer be ignored.

"You'd better have a very good reason for all this, buster," Paula growled as she headed in the direction of Snowball's wails.

For the first time she realized that the cries were coming from Keith's room. She broke into a run, fearing that something terrible was happening in the beautiful little blue-wall-papered nursery.

"When I entered the nursery I was horrified to see that Keith had somehow pulled his mobile down from the edge of the crib and had become tangled in its cords. The more his tiny arms and legs had jerked and kicked to free themselves, the more they had drawn the strings tighter and tighter.

"Keith could not cry out because one of the cords had become wrapped around his neck and was slowly choking him."

Paula swept the containers of powder and the disposable diapers off the changing table as she looked desperately for the nail clippers. Once she had them, she quickly freed her son from the ensnaring cords.

"As I stood there holding Keith in my arms, feeling my heart pound in my chest and watching my baby taking in deep breaths, Snowball jumped up onto the crib rails and began to nuzzle against me," Paula said. "It was as if he were saying, 'Boy, hon, that was one close call. If you ever hear me yelling again, you come running right away!'"

When Stanley came home that night and heard about the close call, he made a "Hero" badge for Snowball out of gold-colored tin foil and pinned it to the cat's collar.

"Snowball was a true hero that day," Paula said. "I will never forget what he did, and I will forever be grateful for the gift he gave us when he saved our son's life."

Elvira Keeps a Half-Naked Baby from Freezing to Death

Greg Harding deliberated for days before he decided to buy a cat for his seven-year-old daughter. In March 1991 he had just reached the point where he could afford to move his family to a quiet suburb of Seattle, and he thought it would be nice if Kimberly had a pet.

But Harding had lost several cats when he was a boy. He would just begin to grow attached to them when they would either wander off and never return or would meet with fatal accidents on the street in front of their home in El Cajon, California. He had come to consider cats unstable, unreliable, perfidious creatures—which were also very accident-prone.

When he brought home Elvira, a young black female, he had a little talk prepared to protect Kimberly's feelings. He told her that cats were more like visitors than permanent members of the family. Cats should be treated with love and respect, but one should never expect them to stay for very long. Kimberly should not be hurt or take it personally if Elvira just upped and disappeared one day.

As the months went by and Elvira turned out to be a regular homebody and a wonderful friend to Kimberly, Harding began to wonder whether the jinx he had always experienced with cats had at last been broken.

"Elvira has brought Kimberly so much happiness," Karen Harding, Greg's wife, said to him one evening. "I'm so happy you were able to rise above your own childhood disappointment in cats."

On the night when Elvira failed to return home, Harding felt he might be guilty of some terrible self-fulfilling prophecy. He stood quietly at the door of Kimberly's bedroom as she asked in her evening prayers for Elvira please to come home to her.

Harding knew well the pain that his daughter felt, and a small voice in the back of his brain kept nagging, "I told you so. Cats never stay."

That night the temperature dropped, and although it seldom snowed heavily around Seattle, enough of the white stuff piled up on the ground to cause Kimberly additional concern for Elvira.

"Elvira will freeze to death, Daddy," she said, fighting back her tears the next afternoon when she came home from elementary school. "We have to go find her."

Harding knew locating a straying cat would be no small job in their area, which was still in the process of being transformed from farms and orchards to houses and yards. A number of rapidly deteriorating barns and outbuildings stood around the area. Elvira could be holed up in any of a hundred places—or she could have been killed by traffic, an unleashed dog, or one of the raccoons that stubbornly hung on to their rapidly vanishing turf.

"Please, Daddy, we have to go out and look for Elvira!"

Karen saw to it that they were both well bundled against the cold, and father and daughter set out in the gathering darkness in search of their missing cat.

In spite of Harding's growing pessimism, after about five minutes of Kimberly's plaintive calling, they seemed to hear answering meows from an old, falling-down barn.

Harding had to keep a firm grasp on his daughter's hand to stop her from running on ahead. He could not risk her stumbling over snow-covered debris or stepping on a rusty nail.

When the two of them finally found Elvira, it was hard to tell which of them was more amazed. The black cat had wrapped her furry self around the half-naked body of a very small baby girl.

"See, Daddy," Kimberly said, smiling through her tears of joy. "Elvira wasn't being naughty by staying out all night. She was taking care of the baby!"

The doctors at a nearby clinic agreed that the deathly pale baby would surely have frozen without the cat's constant attention. The abandoned child, only a few months old, had been kept alive by Elvira's body heat and by her vigorous licking. Thanks to the cat's intervention, "Baby Doe" would recover without any complications.

"Elvira is a hero, isn't she, Daddy?" Kimberly asked on the way home from the clinic, as she hugged the purring cat close. "She couldn't come home if she was going to save the baby girl's life!"

Harding agreed that Elvira must be forgiven for staying out all night without checking in. "Elvira is a hero," he repeated.

Carmel and Bobby—Together Again

Sue Blocher of Brookline, Massachusetts, will always remember that day in September 1977 when her son, Bobby, then four years old, came running up to her in the kitchen where she was busy baking oatmeal cookies and asked breathlessly, "Please, Mommy, oh, please! Can it sleep with me?"

"Can *what* sleep with you? Big Bird? Kermit the Frog? Miss Piggy?"

Bobby giggled. "No, Mommy, no! My kitty. Can my kitty sleep with me tonight?"

Sue arched an eyebrow and wiped a piece of cookie dough off the edge of the bowl.

"But, honey boy," she said, puzzled. "You don't have a kitty."

"I do now, Mommy," Bobby replied confidently. "A pretty *carmel*-colored kitty, just like before. Daddy is bringing her home to me. I saw him buy it."

Darn it! Sue's smile became more like a grimace. Bobby was always doing things like this to her. What did he mean, "a 'carmel-colored' kitty just like before"?

And had he really seen Edward buying him a cat?

Well, she would know the answer to the second question very soon. Her husband was due home from Boston a little after five P.M.

Bobby went out to play, and Sue went back to her cookies.

At 5:08, Edward Blocher pulled into their driveway—with a kitten in the car.

Neither Sue nor Edward had ever seen their son so elated. They were touched by his repeated tearful thank-you's, but bewildered by his triumphant shout, "Oh, yes! It's Bobby and Carmel—together again!"

In the next few weeks, boy and kitten were seldom apart. And they did sleep together every night.

In December Gail, Bobby's baby sister, was born. Bobby and Carmel were at the door to greet her when Sue and Edward brought her home from the hospital.

Gently nudging his Grandmother Linzer aside, Bobby beamed and said to his cat, "See, Carmel. Little Gail. Just like before."

Edward and Sue exchanged puzzled glances, and later that

evening, while they sat at the dinner table talking over the excitement of the day, Sue asked what Bobby had meant by saying, "Just like before."

Bobby shrugged, moving the tip of a finger through a spot of gravy on his plate. "Like before. You know, like before when Carmel, Gail, and I were together."

Edward laughed at his ever-imaginative son, but his mother-in-law glowered at them.

"Such silly talk!" Grandmother Linzer said. "Susan, I've warned you before that you should not permit Robert to chatter on so about such nonsense."

"Mother," Sue reminded the older woman, "Bobby won't be five for another six months. He's a little kid. Little kids sometimes say weird things."

"You never did," her mother said with a sniff. "And remember, as the twig is bent, so grows the branch."

As they were preparing for bed, Sue, fatigued from the birth, asked her husband to pass her the baby *chowder*, rather than the powder.

Edward teasingly reminded her that she never said "weird" things.

Sue laughed. She agreed with her mother's observation that she had been a perfect child, then, turning serious, asked her husband what he made of Bobby's frequent references to "before"—first with Carmel and now with his new sister.

"Maybe he had wanted a cat for so long and so badly that it seemed to him as though he had already had the cat when I finally did bring it to him, and maybe the same thing is true about Gail," Edward said. "Or maybe it's just what you said—Kids say weird things."

Life proceeded on its normal, somewhat hectic course in the Blocher household. Edward received a promotion, and things became more comfortable and less chaotic. They still didn't have enough extra money to allow for more than an occasional night out, but Sue didn't mind, since she hated to leave her children in the care of a baby-sitter.

As for Bobby and Carmel, Sue was convinced that boy and cat communicated on some level beyond the ordinary. At first she had worried that the tight union between Bobby and Carmel would not allow an intruder, but her fears proved unwarranted. Both Bobby and Carmel appeared to adore baby Gail, and they played with her whenever Sue permitted it.

It was just before Bobby's seventh birthday that Sue's and Edward's universe became quite a bit larger.

At quarter to three in the morning, they were awakened by their son's loud weeping. They both ran to his room.

"I don't want Carmel to die," he said between convulsive sobs. "I don't want her to die again!"

The cat looked up at them from her nest in Bobby's bedspread. Her large green eyes appeared to glow in the dim illumination from the Donald Duck night-light near the bedroom door.

"Carmel is fine, Slugger," Edward said softly. "You were just having a bad dream."

"No." Bobby shook his head. "Tomorrow I'll be seven. I don't want Carmel to die like before."

"Bobby, what is this 'before' business again?" Sue asked.

"Like before when the wolf tried to eat Gail! Carmel and I fought and fought to save her, but the wolf killed Carmel— and nearly killed me!"

Edward shook his head and laughed. "Wow! My man, what did you have for a snack before you went to bed? Whatever it was, you are never eating it again!"

Sue stayed at Bobby's bedside, holding his hand until he went back to sleep.

The next afternoon Sue was in the kitchen frosting the birthday cake for Bobby's party.

Her mother was in the backyard with Gail and Bobby.

Edward was still at work, but was expected home any minute.

At 5:30, the Murchisons, the Quateros, and the Fanellis would be bringing their children over for the party.

In Sue's mind, everyone was accounted for, and her world was an orderly place.

What she hadn't counted on was the large German shepherd that had somehow entered their yard.

"Shoo, you dog!" Sue heard her mother scolding. "You don't belong in here, you nasty thing! Get out. Shoo! Shoo!"

Then, as Sue watched in horror through the kitchen window, she saw the shepherd lunge at her mother. Grandmother Linzer screamed, stepped backward, and tripped over a picnic bench—dropping baby Gail.

Sue's mouth opened in a silent scream as her worst nightmare came to life—and she seemed helpless to do anything to stop it. In absolute dread she watched the German shepherd moving toward Gail as if someone had thrown him a tasty chunk of meat.

And then, from out of nowhere, Carmel flew at the big dog's muzzle, scratching, hissing, biting—a veritable guardian angel with claws.

And Bobby was there. Her beautiful, valiant, seven-year-old son was striking at the monstrous dog with the little red plastic baseball bat he had received on his sixth birthday.

"Not like before! Not like before! Not like before!" Bobby chanted in rhythm with the stinging swats he delivered to the snarling dog that threatened his sister.

Bobby's words from the night before echoed in Sue's brain: *"We fought and fought to save her from the wolf!"*

Could it be true? Were Bobby and Carmel fighting the "wolf" all over again?

"Bobby and Carmel—together again!"

The huge dog shook his head vigorously and sent Carmel

flying against the side of the house. The cat was dazed from the blow, but she rolled to her feet and once again advanced on the intruder.

Somehow Bobby had got astride the shepherd and was pulling the dog's ears with all his strength.

The distraction was all Carmel needed. This time, she went for the giant's eyes. She was a demon out of Hell as well as a guardian angel.

The German shepherd shook Bobby off, got the boy on his back, and tried to sink his fangs into Bobby's throat. Bobby cried out in pain as the dog's teeth tore pieces of flesh from his chest.

Her master's screams brought a frenzied power to Carmel's attack. Mercilessly she sank her claws into the dog's left eye.

Emitting terrible yowls of pain, the shepherd tried desperately to shake the screaming cat from its face.

By the time Carmel had once again been thrown against a wall, Sue was there with an iron frying pan. As if Carmel's feline fighting spirit had possessed her, she struck at the big dog's head again and again.

The German shepherd was dazed and barely alive when he staggered from the Blochers' yard. Within the hour, an animal control unit had the dog in custody.

Bobby missed his birthday party. He had to have some stitches and a few shots.

Carmel had a broken back leg that had to be set between splints.

Baby Gail and Grandmother Linzer were unharmed.

And as Bobby said as he hugged his cat on the way home from the veterinarian, "Bobby and Carmel—together again!"

Neither Sue nor Edward asked what he meant. Whether their son had some memory of a past life or had experienced a kind of premonition, it really didn't matter. They only knew for certain that love—whether between human beings or between human beings and animals—lasts forever.

3

KITTY, COME HOME!

In December 1949, Cookie got shipped 550 miles away from her home in Chicago to Wilber, Nebraska, by Railway Express. Six months later, she had managed to find her way back to her old stomping grounds in the Windy City.

In 1953 Chat Beau required four months to hike the nearly 300 miles between his owners' former home in Lafayette, Louisiana, to their new home in Texarkana, Texas.

In 1956 Pooh needed the same amount of time to cover the 200 miles between his human family's former residence in Newnan, Georgia, and their new domicile in Wellford, South Carolina.

Smokey probably rested here and there on his journey from the old homestead in Tulsa to the family's new place in Memphis in 1952; it took him a year to travel those 417 miles.

Tommy required a year and a half to do it, but in 1949 he somehow managed to find his way back home to Seattle from Palo Alto, California—a distance of 850 miles.

In April 1955 Vivian Allgood, a registered nurse, moved from Sandusky, Ohio, to Orlando, Florida, leaving her beloved Li-Ping behind in the care of her sister.

Months later, to Allgood's total astonishment, Li-Ping walked up to her door. The bedraggled cat had somehow managed to travel hundreds of completely unfamiliar miles to find his mistress in a state, neighborhood, and home he had never seen.

Their darling Clementine left the farm in New York to find her family in Colorado. When Clementine's human family moved to Denver in 1949, she was left behind on the farm outside Dunkirk, New York, because she was about to become a mother.

Three months later, her coat rough and matted, her paws cracked and worn, her bushy tail dwindled to a rag, she arrived at the front door of the family's new home in Denver.

How the loving and loyal Clementine had managed to negotiate rivers, mountains, and prairies to find her way to a strange house in a city she had never been to remains a mystery.

Back home again in Indiana. In 1953, when an Army sergeant from Kokomo, Indiana, was transferred to a base near Augusta, Georgia, he decided to take his faithful yellow tomcat with him. Apparently, however, the cat did not take to his new environment; he disappeared almost as soon as the two of them arrived on base. The career soldier spent as much time as he could searching for his pet, then shrugged his loss off as one of the misfortunes of military service.

Three weeks later, the sergeant was astonished when he received a call from friends back in Kokomo who informed him that his yellow tomcat was hanging out around his former home.

The fact that the cat made the return trip so quickly was all the more remarkable to the sergeant's friends when he told them that the critter could not have remembered the route, because he had made the trip to Georgia shut up in a box on an express train.

Maybe they should have explained to Satin about the move. In 1986, when the Tialas moved from Towanda, Pennsylvania, to Forest Lake, Minnesota, a sad mishap occurred. Satin, the object of extreme affection from twelve-year-old Sylvia, escaped from his cage when the family stopped en route at a motel in Illinois.

The family searched the adjacent cornfields for three hours before Sylvia's parents convinced their tearful daughter that they needed to resume their drive to Minnesota.

Many times that winter, the Tialas found their daughter sobbing inconsolably over the loss of her beloved Satin.

Months later, a former neighbor called them with the remarkable news that Satin had returned to their old house in Towanda. The stalwart cat had accomplished his 800-mile odyssey in about eleven months, but he shunned the neighbors and resisted all their efforts to care for him. While Satin would not accept charity, neither would he leave the premises.

The Tialas made the trip back to Towanda to reclaim their wandering cat and to establish him once again as the king of the household and the master of Sylvia's affections.

Tom holds the long-distance record—2,500 miles to find his human family's new home. The long-distance record for a cat finding the way to his or her owners' new home is held by Tom: He accomplished a remarkable 2,500 miles across the continent from St. Petersburg, Florida, to San Gabriel, California, in August 1951.

The seemingly impossible journey took him two years and six weeks, and he arrived much the worse for wear—but he seemed to care only that he was once again united with his human family.

But *Rusty holds the rapid feline flyer record.* In 1949, a cat named Rusty caught up with his human family in Chicago eighty-three days after having become separated from them in Boston. Experts have concluded that Rusty must have found a way to hitch rides on trains, trucks, and automobiles in order to have covered the nearly 1,000 miles in that time.

In *sickness and in health* . . . Misele, Alfonse Mondry's cat, could not bear it when her eighty-two-year-old owner was removed from his farm and taken to a hospital in Sarrebourg, France, in 1991.

What some would term a most remarkable homing instinct, others would call a miracle. Following an infallible guide whose source as yet remains beyond science, Misele set out to visit Mondry in a place she had never been to. With a determination that would not yield to stone quarries, fields, forests, or busy highways, Misele walked the nine miles to the hospital.

Somehow avoiding the orderlies, doctors, and nurses, Misele located Mondry's room, pushed open the door, and jumped onto his bed.

Later that evening, when nurses and doctors found the cat purring contentedly on the old man's lap, they permitted Misele to remain with her master.

Boots *was another cat who could not bear to be separated from her human being.*

In 1990 ninety-two-year-old Leonay Worley was taken to a nursing facility in Davenport, Iowa, twelve miles away from her home.

Worley was delighted when Boots pushed open the door to her room, and the two of them enjoyed a reunion, tearful at least on Worley's part.

Nitpickers pointed out that Boots had visited the nursing

home once before; but she had traveled there in a covered box.

How do they do it? How do cats manage to zero in on their human families wherever they might be? Tales in which a cat finds his or her way *back* to a familiar home over hundreds of miles are remarkable enough, for they seem to reveal some fantastically developed homing instinct. But the accounts of fabulous felines that have traversed unfamiliar and far-distant landscapes to locate their human families in new homes seem to defy all explanation.

Of course skeptics will always exist to declare patronizingly that these people have simply been accidentally "found" by stray cats looking for homes, strays that coincidentally bear a close resemblance to the cats that got left behind. While I cannot deny that such a possibility might explain an occasional case, I have considerable faith in a cat lover's ability to recognize his or her pet.

In the following cases, I rule out any skeptic's proposal of mere coincidence.

Sugar found her way home—in spite of two moves. When the Stacy Woods family decided to move back home to Gage, Oklahoma, from Anderson, California, in June 1951, they thought it would be best to leave their cat, Sugar, with a friend. After all, they had relocated from Oklahoma to California, and now were heading back again, in a brief period. All this moving around, they reasoned, would only confuse their pet.

Fourteen months later, Sugar had found her way back to her human family in Oklahoma.

Although he wanted to welcome Sugar back, Stacy Woods just couldn't believe that a cat would hike—or hitchhike— more than 1,400 miles and find its way home.

But then Stacy recalled that their pet had a deformed hip-bone from an accident in kittenhood. He ran his hand over the feline's flank and found the deformity. The remarkable traveling cat was indeed their Sugar.

*T*he *wonderful oneness of life.* My friends among the traditional Native Americans have no problem with such accounts as the one above, for they believe all life is one. Rather than seeing themselves as having dominion over the beasts, birds, and fish, they see all forms of life as interconnected.

For my friends, the stories of cats that have found their way back to their human families simply show that four-legged entities perceive the lines of connection with their two-legged friends and follow the path the Great Mystery reveals so that they can be together once again.

"This is not 'magic,'" a friend who is shaman of a northeastern tribe explained to me. "It is a power that you use when you have need of it. You see, we are a part of nature and everything is part of one whole. And at the same time, the whole is contained in each part. You are not only a part of the whole, but the whole is part of you."

Traditional shamans, medicine priests, and other Native Americans who follow the old ways so revere all expressions of life that when for whatever reason they must end the existence of an animal, they first utter a prayer, as if performing a sacrament. They believe that both the soul of the individual animal and its group spirit must be told that its physical death is necessary for the turning of the great wheel of life.

Because of the medicine priests' reverence for all the Great Mystery's forms of life, animal as well as human, many early missionaries falsely concluded that the Native Americans worshipped animal idols and a hierarchy of gods.

Human beings who live in open and loving kinship with their pets may develop a sensitivity similar to the harmony with all life that the traditional Native American enjoyed. Modern science is beginning to demonstrate that a distinctive "energy field blueprint" exists around each human being, animal, and form of plant life. Because there appears to be a universality in such electrodynamic field phenomena, we may theorize that on one level every single living cell is connected to every other living cell.

To achieve a nonphysical link or mental communication with family, friends, or pets, a human being may have to separate himself or herself from the demands of physical reality through dreams, visions, meditation or the practice of some technique that encourages an altered state of consciousness. For cats, which deal with many fewer mental, emotional, and cultural demands, it may be a great deal easier to remain spiritually connected with their human family.

Howie Conquers the Australian Outback and 1,000 Miles to Come Home to His Mistress

For fifteen-year-old Kirsten Hicks, the most difficult part of a long overseas family trip in 1977 was having to leave behind her Persian cat, Howie.

In fact, the only people she trusted to look after Howie were her grandparents—and they lived 1,000 miles away from Adelaide, Australia, where Kirsten and her parents lived.

Kirsten was relieved when Grandma and Grandpa readily agreed to take care of Howie for the entire period of her family's absence from Australia. Her grandparents had always liked the magnificent Persian, and they seemed happy at the prospect of having Howie as a house guest. The necessary arrangements were made, and Kirsten happily went off on the long vacation with her parents.

When the Hicks family returned to reclaim Kirsten's furry friend, the grandparents greeted them with the terrible news that Howie had disappeared. They begged their granddaughter's forgiveness and hoped she would understand that they had made every effort to find him.

Kirsten did not hold her grandparents responsible, but she was heartbroken over the loss of her pet. She tried to nurture a feeble hope that Howie might still be alive, but she knew her gorgeous Persian was really a pampered baby and probably wouldn't have lasted five minutes in the streets by himself. He must have been killed by a car or a dog.

Almost exactly a year later, Howie returned to the Hickses' home in Adelaide.

When Kirsten's parents saw the filthy, bleeding, bedraggled cat at their front door, they could not believe their eyes. The thought that the grubby, footsore Persian before them could not possibly be the beautiful Howie passed quickly through their minds.

But Kirsten recognized her feline friend at once. Howie had managed to come home to her. Gently, she picked him up in her arms, and burst into unrestrained tears when she heard his happy purring.

In the twelve months it had taken him to come home, the pampered Persian had somehow forded wild rivers, crossed hostile deserts, and fought his way through the vast wilderness of the Australian outback.

The human imagination boggles at visualizing how the cat could have made his incredible journey. It's perhaps best to leave Howie's homecoming in the category of miracle.

Gribouille Meows, "Vive la France!"

It was nothing personal. Madeleine Martinet of Tannay, France, hoped her cat, Gribouille, would understand, that day in 1987. It was just that she really could not afford to keep a cat, and her neighbor Jean-Paul Marquart was a kind man who would take good care of Gribouille.

Gribouille, we might imagine, shrugged his furry little shoulders with Gallic insouciance. Such things happened, after all. They were really no one's fault. The fellow Marquart set a good table. And besides, Gribouille would be just across the street and could look in on Madeleine from time to time. Life goes on.

But a month later, Marquart upset Gribouille's catnip cart. Gribouille had no idea when he was given to Marquart that the man intended to move from Tannay to Reutlingen, in what was then West Germany.

Hold it here, my friend, Gribouille must have thought. *Deutschland* was not part of the deal! I am a French cat through and through.

Unfortunately, Marquart did not discuss his plans with his newly acquired cat. He packed up his family and moved to Reutlingen, more than 600 miles from Tannay.

There was little that Gribouille could do en route other than complain loudly. Of course, he only got told to be quiet. No one would listen to his side of the matter.

Gribouille barely took time to rest after the trip. He ate one last good meal. Then he set out on the return trek to Tannay.

It took the determined cat two years to cover the 600 miles that separated him from his mistress and his home in France.

When Gribouille reached Madeleine Martinet's doorstep in August 1989, he was starving, bleeding, and nearly blind from a serious infection in both eyes.

Before his ragged body collapsed in her outstretched arms, Gribouille managed to meow.

Martinet must have understand the emotion in that impassioned meow; she told her neighbors that Gribouille was home to stay. She would keep the courageous cat forever.

A few doubting Thomases questioned whether it could possibly be the same cat that had left with Marquart and his family in 1987. If this was truly Gribouille, he would have had to negotiate forests, mountains, rivers, and superhighways. In two years he would have been forced to endure freezing winds and rain, snow and hailstorms, scorching sun and lack of food. Not to mention a thousand angry dogs and two thousand jealous cats that would all have tried to eat him or put out his eyes on nearly every step of the journey.

Madeleine Martinet had a cold look and firm words for all those who dared to deny her Gribouille his miraculous accomplishment.

"There is no doubt that Gribouille is the same cat that left Germany to return to France," she said.

As proof, she cited the fact that the old mother cat that had given birth to Gribouille recognized him at once and began to lick his wounds.

"Gribouille is fit and well now," Martinet said. "And he will stay a French cat forever."

The Return of Rusty

Geoffrey and Sandra Langrish of Camberley, England, were not the first couple to face such a dilemma. Although they were cat lovers and had owned Rusty for quite some time in the summer of 1986, they didn't know whether they wanted to keep him with the baby on the way.

Rusty was a loving cat, but what if he became jealous when Sandra began lavishing attention on the new arrival? One heard so many horrid stories about jealous cats attacking infants, even crawling on their sleeping forms and sucking the breath from their tiny lungs.

And then of course there were the hygienic considerations. Picking cat hair out of the baby's formula, for example. Or what if Rusty brought home some feline disease that could be transmitted to human beings? The baby would be susceptible to such alien germs during its first few months.

Rhoda Young, another cat lover who lived in the next town, heard of the Langrishes' plight and offered to take Rusty off their hands.

Because they had heard about cats that wouldn't stay put in their new homes and somehow found their way back to their former owners, Geoffrey and Sandra put Rusty in a deep basket and covered him with a thick cloth so that he could not possibly see where he was going. They could tell by his nervous movements that he knew something was up, but they managed to keep him covered in the basket until they reached Young's home, sixteen miles away.

Geoffrey and Sandra had barely had time to exchange greetings with Young before Rusty was out the door and gone. It was as if he knew exactly what conspiracy had taken place behind his back, and as soon as the basket was uncovered, he ran between the human beings' legs and disappeared into the village.

Things were tense at the Langrish household for the next few weeks. Nearly every strange sound made them glance toward the cat portal that Geoffrey had set into the kitchen door; they expected to see poor Rusty come staggering into the house, perhaps bloody and beaten, most certainly bedraggled.

And then, of course, there were the attacks of guilt. Rusty had been their faithful cat. How could they have even thought to turn him out?

After a few months with no sign of Rusty, both the hope of his return and the guilt over his disappearance began to fade. The baby arrived, and Sandra and Geoffrey were too busy to think very often of their cat.

And then one day, seven months later, Rusty came walking into the kitchen through his cat portal.

He was none the worse for wear, Geoffrey noticed at once. Rusty had actually gained weight, and he looked the picture of feline health. He was, however, very standoffish, Sandra observed. It was as if he were extremely piqued at having been sent away like a bastard child.

Geoffrey and Sandra wondered where he had been living for the past seven months. He was in much too good condition to have been living paw to mouth in the wild. He must have been boarding with a very attentive cat lover.

As might be expected, Rusty offered no comment that would clear up the mystery. Local animal experts were astounded that he had been able to find his way back home over a route that he had traveled only once before—covered up in a basket.

Rusty seemed only mildly curious about the new addition

to the Langrish family, and Geoffrey and Sandra were so moved by the cat's devotion that they decided not to send him away again to Rhoda Young's place or anyone else's. Rusty would have a home with them as long as he wished to remain.

The Triumphant Homecoming of the Pampered Princess

Ronald and Peggy Keaton of Grand Rapids made no secret of the fact that the whole family pampered Princess, their beautiful calico cat. After all, she was gorgeous and had a sweet disposition, so why shouldn't everyone love her and fuss over her? In fact, Princess had been so sheltered that she had been out of the house only once in her three-year life.

In the winter of 1989, Peggy Keaton's mother, who lived in Toledo, became ill, and Peggy left at once with Ronnie, four years old, and Meagan, two, to stay at the woman's side.

A few days later, Ronald and their six-year-old daughter, Stacy, climbed into the van with the family dog and Princess to make the drive to Toledo. Although it was only the second time in her life that the cat had been out of the house, Ronald didn't want to leave her home alone.

Somewhere between Grand Rapids and Toledo, Princess vanished.

Ronald had made a pit stop at a highway rest area about a hundred miles from home. He was certain Princess was still in the van then because he distinctly remembered having difficulty getting back into the driver's seat because she was up against the window. Stacy got in on the passenger side and moved Princess out of her father's way. Both Ronald and his daughter assumed that the cat moved to the back of the van to find a comfortable spot for a nap.

Ronald did not stop again until he reached his mother-in-law's home in Toledo.

It was then, while they were unpacking the van, that they discovered that their pampered Princess had disappeared.

The three children were distraught. What would happen to their beautiful Princess? They imagined frightening scenes.

Ronald and Peggy believed their delicate house pet would stand a slim chance of survival in the cruel world. After all, they kept needlessly reminding one another, Princess had only been out of the house twice in her entire life.

Certain that their beloved cat would perish in very short order, the Keaton family forced themselves to deal with their grief and focus on the needs of Peggy's ailing mother.

Two nights later, a neighbor back in Grand Rapids telephoned the Keatons to inform them that Princess was sitting on the doorstep of their home, impatiently awaiting their return.

Somehow their pampered, precious Princess had managed to walk the hundred miles back to Grand Rapids in a remarkable three days and return to the right house. Obviously their darling calico was made of much sterner stuff than any of the Keatons had been ready to acknowledge.

The neighbors promised to feed Princess and look after her until the Keatons could come home.

When Ronald and Peggy and the kids returned to Grand Rapids, Princess did not give them a particularly warm welcome. She seemed especially put out with Ronald, Peggy said. "She hissed at him!"

*Mimine Says, "Don't
Start the Vacation
Without Me!"*

Twelve-year-old Bertrand Craye found out that when you develop a close relationship with a cat, the cat expects to be included in all your plans, including your vacations.

In the spring of 1990, Bertrand's parents, Patrice and Michele, decided to visit their vacation home in Le Tourneur, France, and they thought it best to leave Mimine at home with Bertrand's older brother, Gregory.

Bertrand tried his best to explain to the two-year-old tabby that he would soon return.

"Gregory will be kind to you, you'll see," he told Mimine. "And I'll be back before you miss me—too much!"

But when they returned home, Gregory was forced to tell his younger brother that his pet had run away almost as soon as the family had left on vacation.

Bertrand was very upset. He tried hard not to show it, and not to blame Gregory for Mimine's having run away.

The Craye family searched the area extensively, trying their best to locate the straying tabby. After a month, they had to admit that Bertrand's pet was quite likely missing for good.

A few weeks later, to ease the pain of Bertrand's loss, they acquired another tabby and named him Mimine II.

In February 1992, Patrice and Michele Craye returned to their country home in Le Tourneur in the company of Bertrand and Mimine II. They had not been there long when who should come staggering up to the front door, skin and bones, but Mimine I.

It was apparent from the cat's bedraggled appearance that Mimine I had set out for the Crayes' vacation home nearly two years before—and had just arrived.

The persistent pussycat had trudged more than 250 miles across fields, forests, highways, and even the River Seine to reach his young master in Le Tourneur. And he had finally reached his destination, twenty-two months later.

Mimine I responded to Bertrand's tender loving care and a lot of tender morsels of food. He was soon up to his old fighting weight—although he still walked with a limp, a lasting souvenir of some deadly encounter.

He even accepted the presence of Mimine II with style and sophistication. After all, Bertrand had enough love for both of them.

Mimine I had changed in one appreciable way, however. He no longer had the slightest desire to run away from home.

"Please, Mr. Burglar: Bring Back Our Bootsie!"

Everyone knows that some people can simply lose their minds over a certain cat that really appeals to them, but figure this one out.

In March 1992, burglars broke into an electronics specialty

store in Miami and turned their noses up at expensive computer equipment, stereo units, and big-screen television sets. They walked right by about half a million dollars in top-of-the-line electronics without touching a single piece. The sole object of their felonious quest appeared to be Bootsie, a seven-year-old black and white back-alley tomcat.

"It's incredible," exclaimed Benjamin Glumack, the owner of the electronics store. "Whoever broke into my place bypassed hundreds of thousands of dollars' worth of equipment and took only Bootsie, our watchcat, his litter box, about twenty of his toys, his food dish, some snacks, and his bed. And then, as if the burglars' hands got too full, they stole one of our delivery trucks to carry all of Bootsie's stuff!"

Carmilla Schramm, Glumack's bookkeeper, said Bootsie had become the store's mascot. "One of us found him out in the alley all beaten and bloodied. Apparently he had just lost a fight with a pit bull or something. Ben said we could keep him in the back room, and Bootsie had become a fixture around here for about four years."

Glumack said all fifteen of his employees enjoyed having the big black and white tomcat around the store. "Everybody had fallen in love with the guy. Bootsie was lovable. But who would break into the store and risk a jail sentence to steal a lovable cat?"

What puzzled employee Angelina Delpino most about the extraordinary theft was the fact that Bootsie was just an ordinary cat. "He's no expensive, pure-blooded prizewinner. He's no fancy show cat. He's just an old beat-up alley cat with only half his left ear. But we all loved him! Why would anyone steal our cat?"

Glumack said employee morale nose-dived after Bootsie was catnapped. "As weird as it might sound," he said, "I don't care about the delivery truck. They can keep it if they bring back Bootsie."

Kindhearted Widow Fined $750 for Giving Two Stray Kittens a Temporary Home

Can you imagine being fined $750 for feeding a couple of stray kittens? Well, neither could seventy-five-year-old widow Gertrude Cozard, who resided in a plush Savannah, Georgia suburb—and she was fighting mad about it.

"They can lock me up in the penitentiary if they want," Cozard said in May 1991. "I will not pay one cent of my fine. If taking pity on two small kittens is a crime, then they can just put me away in prison."

Cozard's troubles began when she spotted a neighbor pelting two frightened kittens with rocks. It was readily apparent that he had already struck the kittens many times, and one appeared to have suffered a broken leg.

"I had always thought my neighbor to be a cold and inconsiderate person, but such outright cruelty simply appalled me," Cozard said. "The little kittens ran toward my house and hid themselves in the bushes next to my sidewalk. I assumed that they were strays, but that was no reason to treat them so cruelly."

It was against the rules of Cozard's condominium complex to keep pets, but she believed it only humane to give the abused kittens something to eat.

She put out some food by her front door, and she continued to do so for about a week. Touched by the sight of the limping kitten favoring its broken leg, she paid a veterinarian more than $200 to set it.

About that time, she received a telephone call from a man who identified himself as a director of the condominium. He told her that if she continued to feed the kittens he would walk over to her house and personally poison their food. The next few times she fed them, Cozard stood guard over their bowls.

"Within two weeks after I had begun feeding the kittens, I found them a good home with a dear friend who has always loved cats," she said. "I certainly considered the whole matter of the stray kittens to be concluded."

Then she received a certified letter from the condominium board demanding that she reimburse the $750 they had spent in lawyers' fees when they had sought legal counsel on the cat-feeding matter. They also demanded that she sign a legal agreement swearing that she would never again feed a stray animal of any kind.

"Can you believe such a thing?" she asked. "How could anyone sign such a document? Good grief, if a person cannot come to the aid of a couple of helpless kittens, then she is less than human."

Cozard took her story to the newspapers, and animal lovers all over the city wrote to the directors of the condominium to inform them what cruel and heartless monsters they were. This attention, however, only seemed to solidify the board's position.

"We're not going to let her off the hook on this matter," one of them told reporters. "We'll continue this fight to the very end."

In the meantime, Cozard hired an attorney of her own to battle the condominium board in court, and she put her $200,000 home on the market. Although the legal battle has been met with delays and remains unresolved, she still believes in her cause.

"I cannot live around evil people who hate animals," she said.

What if All the Kitties Came Home at Once?

For the first time in the history of the United States, cats are more popular than dogs.

There are an estimated 53.3 million dogs in American households, and 62.4 million cats. Nearly two in five households own a dog, while one in three includes a cat.

In 1991, the International Cat Association licensed 243 shows—including the largest, New York's International Cat Show, held in Madison Square Garden. Dozens more were sponsored by other cat fanciers' associations.

And while there is no question that Americans love their cats, they come in second to the people of Australia as the world's greatest cat lovers. According to *Petfood Industry* magazine, 33 percent of all families in Australia fancy felines, followed by 30 percent in the United States. After the U.S., the Canadians and the Belgians place third and fourth in their passion for pussycats.

Unlike dogs, many of which are bred to improve their performance as retrievers, shepherds or watchdogs, cats are bred only for their looks and their temperament.

For cat lovers, beauty, grace, and a pleasant disposition are quite enough. It is not necessary for a feline pet to be able to sound an alarm, fetch downed birds, herd domesticated livestock, or attack burglars.

To be a cat lover is to be enraptured by that mysterious mixture of wild beast and otherworldly being that constitutes a feline.

To be a cat lover is to hold that bizarre blend of the ethereal and the earthy in such respect that you cannot help feeling honored when your cat jumps into your lap.

It seems that even the process of breeding cats is a deeply satisfying experience that surpasses all physical considerations—since recent statistics disclose that half of all these devoted breeders are allergic to cats.

To non-cat lovers, it might seem that some people get more than a little carried away by their obsession with felines.

When Christine Ann Thomas's husband told her, "It's either me or the cats," the cat-loving fanatic—note her initials—didn't even pause to think. She chose her cats—all 129 of them.

So in December 1991, Billy, her husband of sixteen years, moved out of their home in Wakefield, England; and he vowed that he would not return until the dozens of cats his wife had adopted hightailed it out of the house.

Christine would not back down. "By leaving, Billy has simply created more room for me to take in cats," she said.

Jack and Donna Wright of Kingston, Ontario, own 600 cats that regularly come close to eating them out of house and home.

In January 1992, the Wrights were threatened with eviction when they were unable to pay their mortgage after having spent $111,000 a year on their beloved pets. When cat lovers from Kentucky to Winnipeg learned of their plight, they rallied to the cause and sent Jack and Donna enough donations to help them regain their financial equilibrium.

Each day the Wrights feed their hosts of felines 180 cans of cat food, 50 pounds of dry cat food, and nine quarts of milk—which adds up to $256 a day, including kitty litter. In addition, they have a veterinarian in every day, at an average of $50 a visit. That's a total of $306 a day—$2,142 a week.

The Wrights believe that every penny spent on their cats is worth it. "We love each and every one of our six hundred cats," they said. "Our cats are like our children. We'll never let anyone take them away from us."

When representatives of the Toronto Humane Society answered a call for help in the summer of 1990, they found a couple in their seventies attempting to care for 160 cats in a cramped three-bedroom apartment.

Humane Society investigator Martha Schissler said the couple were trying their best to care for the animals and that all the cats were quite well fed.

"In such numbers, however, it was impossible for the elderly couple to care for them properly," Schissler said. "They finally permitted me to take eighty-nine of the cats, but they insisted on keeping seventy-one of their favorites."

Martha Richardson of Nashville will never have to worry about her more than 1,000 cats eating her out of house and home. Her precious pussycats are salt shakers, dolls, statues, bookends, photographs, paintings, and a seemingly endless variety of collectibles.

Richardson said she stopped counting at 1,000 pieces. "There isn't a place in my house where you can go without being stared at by a cat painting, sculpture, towel, or stuffed cat. Every nook and cranny is crammed with cat collectibles peeking out from every corner."

The first item she collected was a small stuffed cat doll she received as a child. She now possesses an almost endless array of cat art pieces from more than forty countries, including a cat likeness she wears attached to her thumbnail.

It should surprise no one to learn that she sends out cat Christmas cards—with cat stamps, of course.

4

THE TOUGH GUYS—CATS WITH MORE THAN NINE LIVES

In the winter of 1990, Snowball, a white Angora kitten owned by Carol Gingras of Middleborough, Massachusetts, took a two-foot arrow through the head from a sicko sadist and recovered.

In January 1990, Kelly, a once tubby tabby owned by Rhea Mayfield of Brownwood, Texas, was found alive after having been locked in an storeroom for forty-six days without food or water—in below-zero cold.

Putty Cat, an eleven-pound tom, loves to soar with the birds on a hang glider with his mistress, Patty Butler. Butler has created a special harness so that Putty Cat need never miss a flight off the cliffs near Monterey, California.

In the summer of 1992, Jerry Ditzig of Highlands, Texas, was doing speed laps before going on to win the Bud Lite International Outboard Grand Prix in Missouri. When he pulled in for a pit stop, he heard a tiny mewing sound and pulled off the engine cover to investigate.

There, to his astonishment, he discovered two tiny kittens,

63

barely three weeks old. The stowaways, one snow-white, the other black with white paws, were soaked.

Since his wife is a "cat nut," Ditzig decided to adopt the kittens, naming them Speed and Racer in recognition of the fact that they started life doing 103 mph in a racing powerboat.

Vision Spends Six Weeks in a Dresser Drawer

Vision, a three-year-old orange, black and white tabby, got trapped in a dresser drawer in August 1991, when the Williams family moved from Fort Meade, Maryland, to Lantana, Florida; she survived forty-two days without food or water.

Barbara Williams said she was puzzled when she thought she heard a weak meowing coming from a drawer in the dresser, which they had stored in a warehouse. "I couldn't believe Vision was alive," she said.

Before their departure to Florida, after movers in Maryland had packed the family belongings, the Williamses had discovered that Vision was missing. After searching the neighborhood for a week, they had sadly concluded that she must have become upset by the chaos of moving and run away to find a new home.

It was a full six weeks after their arrival in Florida before the Williamses could unpack some of the furniture they had stored, and poor Vision was stuck in the dresser drawer all that time.

The examining veterinarian said Vision's survival was all the more spectacular considering that the Florida warehouse had no air-conditioning. Vision had suffered some dehydration, but the vet said, "She's in terrific shape for what she's gone through. We were all stunned that she was able to survive."

Sometimes a Dog's Best Friend Is a Cat

In 1957 Bos'n, a large gray tomcat belonging to the J. R. Rowntrees of Mill Valley, California, suddenly dashed from the house when he spotted their cocker spaniel, Duke, wandering out of the yard. Duke had gone blind because of cataracts and was heading for a steep incline and a bad fall. Nudging the old dog along on either side, Bos'n brought him safely home.

On October 17, 1990, Teresa Harper had just let her poodle, Lacy Jane, out into the yard of her home in Dora, Alabama, when the tiny dog was attacked by a massive pit bull that had invaded the Harpers' property.

Lacy Jane was being severely mauled when her pal Sparky, the Harpers' cat, leaped from the roof of a nearby porch to land squarely on the head of the savage pitbull. Four-pound Sparky drove off the vicious dog and saved the poodle's life.

In the fall of 1968, a tomcat named Thug received an award for heroism from the Los Angeles Society for the Prevention of Cruelty to Animals after rescuing a dog. Normally an exceptionally quiet cat, Thug spotted a Labrador retriever being swept under a pier at a marina. The tom began a series of alarming yowls that drew attention to the dog's peril, and Missy the Labrador was saved.

In August 1987, a tiger-striped New England barn cat came to the support of her female collie friend as the dog desperately defended her newborn pups from a powerful and hungry predator.

Richard Olson, who maintains a large farm near Fort Dodge, Iowa, thought Queenie, his white collie, was secure with her five new pups in an old corncrib.

"The family and I were going into town that night to see a movie," Olson said. "The girls were reluctant to leave Queenie, since she was still kind of weak and woozy from having given birth only the night before, but they fixed a nice bed for her made up of some old worn-out blankets; and we saw to it that she was as comfortable as any mother could be who was nursing five new babies."

When the family returned home around eleven o'clock that night, they were horrified to see Queenie outside the corn crib, staggering near exhaustion. In the illumination of the yard light, they saw splotches of blood staining her white coat.

They had little time to puzzle over what had happened to their collie, for in the next few minutes something came running at her from out of the shadows and knocked her sprawling. It was a huge muskrat that must have come up from the nearby creek to get at the tender newborn pups.

"Get Dad's rifle from the kitchen closet!" Olson's wife shouted at their older son.

Olson was afraid it might be too late to stop the muskrat from its savage onslaught. He was too far away from the corncrib to chase the animal away, and it looked as though Queenie was down and out.

That was when another shadowy figure rose from the doorway of the corncrib to meet head-on the determined charge of the hungry muskrat. It was Meower, the Olsons' New England barn cat. She caught the predator with a raking slash of her claws across its nose.

"You could probably have heard that muskrat squeal all the way back in town," Olson said. "Meower stood there, poised like a prizefighter, jabbing and thrusting at the huge muskrat with drawn claws. Meower's delaying tactic gave Queenie time to regain her breath and her balance, and Queenie got that muskrat behind its neck, shook it violently several times, then tossed it as far as she could throw it.

"The muskrat rolled about seven or eight feet into the darkness, rebounded on its feet, and came running back for another try at the puppies. It was tough and mean—and it was hungry for fresh meat."

By that time Olson's son had brought the .22 rifle, and Olson nailed the muskrat with three quick shots.

"The grass outside of the corncrib door was all torn up," he said. "Queenie must have smelled the muskrat outside the crib and knew darn well the purpose for the critter's visit. Although she was weak from having given birth only the night before, she positioned herself outside to keep the invader away from her pups.

"Old Meower, who's got to be over ten years old, must have seen that her pal Queenie was getting the worst of it in her weakened condition and all, so she planted herself right in the doorway of the crib and stood there prepared to fight to the death to protect Queenie's babies. If it hadn't been for the reinforcements of Meower's sharp claws, Queenie would undoubtedly have lost a pup or two."

Igor the Tabby Takes on Two Coyotes to Save a Siamese

In June 1991, when Connie and Dennis Junagan moved to the newly developed desert housing units outside Cave Creek, Arizona, they did not fully comprehend that in this particular region the West was still wild. Their two kids, Patti, eleven, and Bruce, nine, lived in dread of whatever might be the creepy-crawly of the day. The family cat, Igor, a large gray tabby, suddenly found himself the possible diet of choice for a large variety of predators.

"Within the first week of our move, we had encountered a six-foot-long rattlesnake on our driveway, a scorpion in our dishwasher, four or five lizards in our bathroom, two hairy tarantulas on our patio, a pack of six coyotes in our backyard, and a herd of thirteen javelina, wild pigs, in our front yard," Connie Junagan said. "We were continually concerned about the kids being bitten by any one of the above—and about Igor, who we feared might try to tease in a catfully playful manner some poisonous creature or other."

One feature of their new surroundings, the mournful moonlight dirge of the coyotes, the Junagans found strangely satisfying. But then they found out how wily those coyotes could be.

"Our next-door neighbors actually had their cocker spaniel eaten by a pack of coyotes," Dennis said. "The coyotes will cleverly send a female in heat up to homes in which they can detect dogs dwelling within. When the horny hound goes out in pursuit of the fertile lady, the pack of male coyotes jump him and eat him."

The Junagans also learned that the coyotes loved nothing better for a midnight snack than a cat that didn't make it home before dark.

"So many things in life present a mixed blessing," Dennis said. "Although there was a definite threat to Igor, Patti and Bruce suddenly became much more responsible in terms of seeing that their pet was home safely. In our old neighborhood in Paradise Valley, Arizona, they had been pretty lax about whether or not Igor was home behind doors after dark."

Dennis commented with a wry smile that he had always known Igor was a "ballsy" cat, reluctant to back down before the most aggressive dogs in the neighborhood, but somehow the big tabby had to understand that coyotes were much hungrier than the average urban mutt. As his son Bruce had phrased it, Igor's hero had always been Garfield, the pugilistic tiger cat in the Sunday comics.

It was Patti who actually witnessed Igor's act of heroism.

"Elise, who was nine and who lived next door, and I were playing dolly dress-up with our cats in our backyard," Patti said. "Elise had pulled a pink dolly sundress on Sara, her Siamese, and I was trying to put a yellow apron around Igor's big belly. We didn't even see the two coyotes until they were right in front of our noses, growling at us and showing their teeth."

Although their parents had warned Elise and Patti about the boldness of coyotes in invading garages and yards, the adults had never anticipated that the scavengers of the desert would have the audacity to approach human beings, even little ones such as their daughters.

Patti said later that Sara, Elise's Siamese, had started yowling and hissing at the uninvited guests, but that Igor had just studied the intruders closely, as if looking for an opening.

Sara's defiance either provoked one of the coyotes or stimulated his hunger; he lunged at the Siamese and snatched her up in his jaws in one practiced swoop. That was when Igor went into action.

"He made a really big jump and landed on the head of the coyote that had grabbed Sara," Patti said. "The coyote dropped Sara and shook Igor off. Then Igor went right for its face, making a terrible howling while he scratched and scratched at the coyote's nose.

"The coyote yelped so loud that both of them turned and ran from the yard. Igor was a big hero!"

Sara required a number of stitches at the veterinarian's, but she was not much the worse for wear by dinnertime that evening. Elise's parents brought Igor a can of expensive cat food as a gift for saving their daughter's pet.

"Igor really thinks he's Garfield," Bruce said. "He really thinks he can take on all comers!"

Mercedes Stows Away Without Food or Water for Fifty Days

Although the good-natured employees at the freight company in Kent, England, had been feeding the stray black cat bits and pieces of their lunches for the past few weeks, none of them probably thought much of it when the feline moocher stopped coming around. And it's doubtful that any of them would have associated the disappearance of the black cat with their shipping a Mercedes-Benz to a woman in Australia.

As remarkable as it may seem, on that day in 1990 when the employees of the freight company were in the process of sealing the metal container which was to protect the expensive automobile en route to Australia, they also enclosed the black cat in what might well have been her seagoing tomb.

The unwilling feline stowaway—who came to be called Mercedes—survived fifty days without food or water, locked securely in the shipping container.

In an unparalleled feat of endurance, Mercedes traveled 17,000 miles in her metallic crypt. When the ship arrived in Port Adelaide, Australia, nearly two months later, customs officials were stunned when the skin-and-bones cat stumbled out.

Dr. John Holmden, a veterinarian and chief animal quarantine officer in South Australia, theorized that Mercedes must have had a full stomach before she became trapped in the container. By licking drops of condensation and by spending nearly all of her time resting, she managed to stay alive.

When Mercedes staggered out of the container, she barely weighed four pounds. After being fed plenty of cat food and a lot of milk, she soon filled out to eight pounds, quite likely her former weight.

Under Australia's strict quarantine laws, Mercedes had to be detained for nine months. After her release from quarantine, the owner of the Mercedes-Benz announced that she intended to adopt the feisty orphan cat that had shared the metal container with her automobile from Kent to Port Adelaide.

Buried Alive for Eleven Days, Marty Digs Himself Free

Marty probably got himself in trouble while pursuing his favorite pastime—chasing mice into holes around the patio of the Dunbars' apartment building in Edina, Minnesota.

What most likely occurred on the afternoon of April 9, 1992, is that Marty felt a little shy when the maintenance men came around to work on the patio, and found a hole big enough to hide his yellow-striped body. Of course Marty had no idea that the workmen would place a ten-inch slab of patio concrete over his hiding place.

Eight-year-old Frankie Dunbar was inconsolable when Marty had not come home after three days. He had received Marty on his fifth birthday, and they had become fast buddies.

"I want to see my kitty again," Frankie sobbed to his mother, Robin. "When is Marty going to come home?"

When Frankie's father, Greg, returned from work on the fourth day after Marty's disappearance, the three members of the Dunbar family scoured the neighborhood calling for the cat. Later, after dinner, they posted reward notices in all the supermarkets within a reasonable cat-hike from their apartment building.

On the evening of the ninth day, Robin and Greg sat Frankie between them on the sofa and explained about death and about how, just maybe, Marty had had an accident and wouldn't be coming home. Frankie cried himself to sleep.

Eleven days later, on Easter Sunday, Marty appeared at the Dunbars' patio door.

"He was covered with dirt," Robin Dunbar said. "His paws were so muddy it looked like he was wearing miniature boxing gloves."

"We were astonished," Greg admitted. "Speechless. We could only blurt out half-sentences like 'Look there . . . there he is . . . Marty. Look. Marty has come back.' "

Frankie was overjoyed to see his pet, but Marty didn't stand on ceremony. He headed straight for his food bowl and began to eat, apparently trying to gain back in one meal the weight he had lost.

When Greg and Jerry Faciana, the maintenance supervisor at the Dunbars' apartment complex, found the hole in the lawn, they began to reconstruct the circumstances of Marty's disappearance and his return.

"We think he must have crawled into a hole near the patio on the day when the workmen were patching the area with new stones and concrete," Greg Dunbar said. "He probably hid from them, and they poured a slab of concrete right over the place where he lay crouched in his hole.

"Once he realized he was trapped, Marty probably started trying to dig himself out. We figure he must have stayed alive by burrowing into pockets of mice as he dug."

Jerry Faciana commented about the condition of Marty's paws. "The poor guy didn't have any claws left at all. He had worn them down to nothing from scratching his way to freedom."

Frankie asked his parents whether Marty had used up all of his nine lives in his escape.

"Marty has always been a fighter," Greg told him. "I'll just bet he saved at least one or two lives for future emergencies."

Tomcat Frozen to a Tree Is Rescued by Six Cat Lovers

Teresa Bishop was on her way home from her job at a local hospital on the evening of March 2, 1991, when she stopped her car near a wooded embankment outside St. Catharines, Ontario.

"It was already dark, but I simply needed a good breath of fresh air," Bishop said. "I had put in a really tough day, and I just needed to stop and look up at the stars and feel the chill wind against my face."

The wind was indeed chilly; the temperature was about four degrees below zero.

As Bishop stood quietly, she heard a faint sound, a kind of whimpering, that seemed to be coming from about halfway down the wooded embankment.

Drawn by the sound, she began to edge her way down through the snow-covered undergrowth. "Even at the time I understood that I could certainly have slipped and hurt myself badly," she said.

"At the very first, I couldn't quite identify what the sound was. It was now quite dark, and it took me about half an hour to pinpoint that the cries were coming from an uprooted spruce tree. After a time of hearing the cries regularly, I knew that there had to be a cat in trouble somewhere in that tree."

Bishop carefully inched along the trunk of the fallen tree, holding the branches for support. Again the thought occurred to her that she might fall and be injured there in the darkness. How long would it be before someone came to *her* rescue?

And then, suddenly, her groping fingers found the cat, its hind legs and tail firmly frozen to the spruce tree.

"I knew that unless I got the cat out of there in a hurry, it would soon be frozen to death," Bishop said. "The poor thing had almost no body heat left, and with the temperature below zero, it couldn't hold out much longer."

Desperately she tried to dig the cat free from the ice with her fingernails.

"The ice seemed as hard as iron, and I knew I did not have the strength to chip him free with my nails," she said.

"The cold was starting to get to me, and I was losing my grip on the branches that kept me from falling. I knew I would be no good to the cat or anyone, including myself, if I slipped in the darkness and lay helpless beside the tree trunk."

Bishop climbed safely back to the highway and her automobile and was soon revving the car's engine and racing to find help for the frozen kitty.

Officers Harry Frizzell and Al Rand followed her back to the embankment. Frizzell tried to chip the animal free with his knife without success. Rand poured antifreeze around the cat, but that didn't work either.

Three more officers, touched by the cat's plight when they heard Frizzell discussing it over the radio, arrived in a cruiser with two jugs of hot water.

"There were six of us there in the dark and the freezing cold when the hot water worked and thawed the ice around the imprisoned cat," Bishop said, "and all of us had tears in our eyes when he was free at last."

Amid expressions of goodwill and congratulations, Bishop took the cat home with her.

"After several bowls of warm milk and a couple of poached

eggs, his body temperature became normal," she said, "and that was when I knew that we had truly saved the cat's life."

Because of the strict rules against pets in her apartment building, Bishop was unable to keep the cat, which she nick-named Frosty, but she found a home for him with a loving family.

"I will always cherish the memory of that magical night when six busy humans ceased worrying about their own prob-lems and concerns and focused their energy on saving the life of one small tomcat that was frozen in a tree," Bishop wrote in her account of the incident. "I think we all got a good lesson in the oneness of all life that night."

Roxanne the Rambo Kitty Keeps Neighborhood Dogs in Check

When Michael and Elaine Claussen moved to their new neighborhood in Albany, New York, in 1989, they were aston-ished by the laxity of dog owners who failed to keep their pets in check.

"Complaining brought apologies and promises to keep Fido on a leash," Elaine said, "but it just never happened."

"The doggie-do in the yard and on the sidewalk was one thing," Michael added, "the urine stains on the tires and fence posts were another—but I planted two rosebushes, then lost them to the mutts within the first four days after we moved into the neighborhood."

The Claussens had lived there only a month when their daughter Linda asked them to take care of her cat, Roxanne, a cross-bred tabby and Persian. At first the couple hesitated to assume responsibility for Linda's big brown cat. After all, the neighborhood was crawling with dogs. What if one of them injured or killed Linda's beloved companion?

"The other reason for our hesitation, quite frankly," Michael said, "was that I was allergic to cats. And besides that, I had never really cared for the things."

The Claussens finally consented to take Roxanne for the next two weeks, and Linda dropped the cat off on her way to the airport.

"You'll pardon me if I leave the care and keeping of this big mama primarily to you, dear," Michael said to Elaine, reaching for his handkerchief. "My allergy, you know."

The next afternoon, Elaine was ironing and listening to Beethoven on the stereo when she glanced out the kitchen window and spotted a large German shepherd boldly approaching Roxanne, who was sunning herself in the backyard.

" 'Oh, no,' I thought to myself. 'Poor Roxanne is about to be converted into hamburger,' " Elaine said. "Michael was at work, and I was very cautious about running afoul of an angry German shepherd. I was already trying to decide what I would tell Linda when she returned from her vacation."

Roxanne barely opened her sleepy eyes, reached up and expertly raked the shepherd's nose with the extended claws on her left paw. The dog ran yelping from the yard.

Within a few days, it became abundantly clear that Roxanne was the equal of any dog in the neighborhood. Cocker spaniels, poodles, and beagles were easy knockouts, and she barely ruffled her fur taking out the mean rottweiler from around the corner and the German shepherd, which returned for a rematch.

"It's amazing," Michael laughed when he returned from work on the fourth day of Roxanne's visit. "The dogs in the neighborhood are starting to avoid coming near our yard. Old Slugger Roxy is scaring them all away. I think I'll try planting rosebushes again."

On Saturday afternoon, the seventh day of the reign of Queen Roxanne, Michael was able to observe their Rambo cat in action as he tamped the soil around a freshly planted rosebush.

"This big rottweiler approached our yard," he said. "I had seen the brute in the neighborhood, and I knew I wouldn't want to tangle with him. He walked up to the edge of our grass, and he had this low, throaty growl building in his throat.

"Without a moment's hesitation, Roxanne jumped up from where she had been napping beside me and came hissing and spitting at the big rottweiler. The monster backed up, but then decided to stand his ground. That was when Roxy moved deftly between his front legs and sank her fangs up to the hilt in one of his back legs. The brute yelled all the way back to his own yard around the corner."

That night, Michael gave Roxanne an extra helping of her favorite mixture of cheese and tuna, then conducted a formal weighing-in on the bathroom scale.

"It might not be official," he told Elaine, "but our champ tips the scales at nearly twenty-five pounds. No wonder she has no fear. She knows she's the biggest, meanest pussycat in the valley."

On the tenth day of Roxanne's stay with the Claussens, Elaine noticed that for the first time since they had moved to the neighborhood the dog owners were walking their pets on leashes. She also observed that most of the dogs whimpered as they were tugged past the edge of the Claussen's front lawn.

"Roxanne has all the neighborhood dogs running scared," Elaine reported to Michael that evening when he came home from work. "Now nearly everyone has their dog on a leash, and Mrs. Myer from across the street called to see if Roxanne was inside the house before she would walk her dog."

Michael bent down to give Roxanne an affectionate scratch behind the ear. For some reason, his allergy to cats no longer seemed to bother him.

"Roxanne is like Marshal Dillon cleaning up Dodge City," he said, chuckling. "Roxy has the fastest claws in the West."

The next morning when he was leaving for work, Michael was amused to see that some neighborhood wit had placed a crude "Beware of the Cat" sign next to their front walk.

When the two weeks of Linda's vacation were up and she stopped by to pick up her "sweet little kitty," Michael told his daughter she could have Roxanne back only if she promised to bring her over for a visit every few weeks.

The Cat That Was Mistaken for a Terrorist Bomb

Thunderball was forced to surrender at least eight of his nine lives all at once when he had the misfortune to be sealed in a cardboard box and left in front of a government building. The frightened feline accomplished a miraculous escape when the box was blown up by an Army antiterrorist squad who had mistaken it for a bomb.

The terrible mishap occurred in early February 1991, at the peak of the Persian Gulf conflict. Rumors abounded that Iraqi terrorists had pinpointed numerous U.S. cities for reprisals, and law enforcement agencies across the country were extra vigilant.

For some bizarre purpose, a person or persons unknown stuffed a kitten and some pieces of fried chicken into a two-foot-square box filled with old newspapers and sealed it. A note which said only "To Suzy" was attached to the box, and the package was left outside a government building in a major Southern city.

At around six A.M., Sheriff Charles Herbert received a report from two patrolling deputies that they had spotted a mysterious box in the driveway between the county courthouse and the jail.

"It's right in the middle of the courthouse's loop driveway," one of the officers told him. "It could be a bomb that a terrorist has left to go off during business hours."

Local police roped off the area, and a bomb squad was summoned from a nearby Army base.

Sheriff Herbert was told to evacuate the jail, but he had no idea where he could put 400 inmates in a matter of minutes.

The Army bomb squad could detect no sound issuing from the box, so they made a decision to blow the top off the package.

Within moments, the air was filled with shredded newspaper and bits of fried chicken.

"Seconds later," Deputy Sheriff Mark Pickett said, "all of us onlookers were startled to hear the sounds of frightened mewing coming from the smoking box. Then, before our stunned eyes, a badly injured kitten started to crawl out of the box. It looked around at us, shook its head as if to shake out echoes of the explosion, then limped beneath a nearby car."

Deputy Pickett retrieved the kitten from under the automobile and immediately made the decision to adopt him. "The name Thunderball seemed very appropriate," he said.

Veterinarian Dr. Cathy Seale removed Thunderball's left

rear leg and treated his lungs and mutilated tail. "It was a miracle that Thunderball was still basically in one piece," she said. "With that resiliency that is common among cats, I could see that he would pull through."

Deputy Pickett said Thunderball was an exceptionally sweet kitten. "You'd think he might be full of mistrust and anger toward humans after what happened to him, but he plays happily with me, my wife, and our two other cats."

"Thunderball was the innocent victim of the Iraqi terrorism scare that swept our country during the Persian Gulf conflict," Sheriff Herbert said. "We feared we might have a bomb in the box, but all we had was a harmless little kitten and some pieces of fried chicken."

Ronald's Car Ride from Hell

On the morning of July 17, 1992, Estelle Littmann of Montgomery, Alabama, was in her station wagon on her way to the bank where she had worked as a teller for more than eleven years. She was only a few miles from her home when she was startled by a man in a brown van who pulled up beside her and began to shout and wave wildly.

"I was frightened," Littmann said. "You hear all the time about killers and maniacs trying to assault women on the highways. At first I tried to ignore him."

But the man in the van pulled ahead of her, flashed his signal lights, and motioned for her to pull over.

"I thought, 'No way am I going to pull over and become the next victim of some serial killer,' " she said.

"I floored the accelerator and shot around him at top speed. I was, in fact, driving about fifteen miles over the speed limit, hoping that some cop would spot me on his radar and come to arrest me and to save me."

When her persistent pursuer caught up to her once again, Littman had another thought. Perhaps this was all connected to her position with the bank. She remembered seeing a movie or a television special about some bank robbers who first kidnapped bank personnel and then forced them to assist in the theft.

At last she spotted a housing development where a security guard was stationed. She felt certain that if she drove up to the guard on duty, the nutcase following her would flee.

As she pulled into the driveway by the guard's station, the man in the brown van honked his horn several times and drove on.

"I thought the pervert had to give me one last beep on his horn," Littmann said, "but I didn't care if he thought he was insulting me or not. At last I was rid of him."

The security guard stepped out of his station to ask what she wanted, and she watched his face turn pale.

"Ma'am," he blurted out, "you got a cat on the top of your car!"

Littmann quickly unbuckled her seat belt and pushed open the door of the station wagon. Her mouth dropped open, and she knew she was turning several shades paler than the security guard.

"There, on top of my station wagon, spread-eagled on the roof and clutching onto the luggage rack for dear life, was my black and white tomcat, Ronald!" she said. "The poor baby had just had the ride from Hell, and he looked like he was frozen solid in complete and total fear."

Littmann said it took two or three days of lots of tender loving care to "unthaw" Ronald, but he was soon doing fine, none the worse for his ride of terror on the top of a speeding car.

The Pussycat "Frozen with Fear" Was Really a Gargoyle Made of Stone

Although the following story may sound like a Monty Python sketch, in 1991 a tipsy cat lover in Brighton, England, fell thirty feet from an office building when he tried to rescue a kitty that was actually a stone gargoyle.

The young man was out with friends celebrating his twenty-third birthday when he spotted what he was certain was a frightened cat clinging to the outside of a three-story building.

"There's no question about it," he said valiantly. "Duty calls. I must scale the wall, and I must rescue that poor, trembling, terrified cat."

"I should think there is a bit of risk involved," one of his friends said, seeking to dissuade him. "The poor thing looks awfully high up. Perhaps we should call the fire department or the humane society or some such professional cat rescuers."

"The danger inherent in climbing to a great height is certainly no reason to shirk one's responsibility to humane and noble deeds," the stewed-to-the-gills Galahad decreed.

"If I'm seeing what you're seeing, old sport," another friend commented, squinting up at what appeared to be a feline form hugging the building for dear life, "that is not a real cat, but rather a stone gargoyle. You know, the ugly creatures they put on buildings to frighten away evil spirits and all that sort of rubbish."

"You've had far too much to drink," the birthday celebrant scolded his pal. "Imagine mistaking a poor frightened pussycat for a wretched gargoyle on Notre Dame Cathedral or something. You should go home if you're going to carry on so."

Shaking himself free of his friends' restraining hands, the tipsy rescuer began to climb the side of the office building, carefully wedging fingers and shoe soles into every available crack between the bricks and stones.

"I am going to rescue that cat," he announced to the world in general and to his fellow celebrants in particular. "I shall be its hero. My name shall be honored among cat lovers throughout the world."

But before the highly inebriated cat fancier could reach the lifelike sculpture, he lost his grip and fell thirty feet to the pavement, fracturing his skull.

Later police authorities commented that the would-be rescuer, who was recovering in the hospital, had said he'd been convinced that the stone cat wasn't moving because it was "frozen with fear." He was now willing to concede, however, that it must have been a stone gargoyle, content to remain on constant vigil against demons attacking the building, not a real-life, flesh-and-blood feline in distress.

Smokey Endures Thirty-seven Days in an Empty Vending Machine

Laura Dalfonso had had her smoky gray Siamese for a little over a year when he disappeared in July 1990.

"I was heartbroken," Dalfonso said. "I own a vending machine business in a suburb of Baton Rouge, Louisiana; and I had gotten into the routine of taking Smokey everywhere with me on my rounds. He sat on a pillow next to my chair when we watched television, and he rode on my lap whenever we would go anywhere in the car."

Dalfonso spent the days after Smokey disappeared searching the neighborhood and tacking up reward posters in all the malls and supermarkets.

"I got to thinking that I had sold six vending machines to Martin Napier the day Smokey had disappeared," Dalfonso said, "and I started getting a feeling that Smokey might have somehow got inside one of those machines."

Napier was sympathetic when she phoned him. Although she said she doubted Smokey could actually be hiding in a vending machine, Napier promised to go out to his warehouse and check them right after he hung up.

"I did check them out just as I promised," he said. "But I didn't open them up and look inside. After all, every slot and opening was closed, so I couldn't see any way on earth a cat could have wriggled between a hairline crack and got inside. Besides, I put my ear to every one of those machines to listen for anything that sounded like a cat, and there were no strange sounds coming from any of them."

Dalfonso continued her lonely quest, taping up hundreds of "lost cat" signs and walking through the woods and nearby neighborhoods calling Smokey's name. After thirty days, she gave up hope that she would ever see Smokey again.

Martin Napier was beginning to prepare his vending machines for service. A local school board had bought all six, and it was almost time to install them for the fall term.

"You could have knocked me over with a feather when I opened up the fourth machine and saw these big blue eyes looking up at me from a scruffy cat face," Napier said. "It was Laura's cat, Smokey, all right. Somehow he had managed to get himself hidden away in a compartment that was nineteen by thirty inches—and only eight inches high."

Napier put his hand out, and Smokey rubbed his head against the man's palm.

"It was obvious that the cat was just too weak to even stand up," he said. "I rushed him to a veterinarian, who told me that Smokey had probably lost about half his weight through dehydration and malnutrition."

Dr. Carla Rhea admitted that thirty-seven days without food or water was an amazing feat of endurance, but she added that cats seem to have the ability to go for long periods without nourishment of any kind.

When he was certain Smokey would be all right, Napier called Laura Dalfonso and gave her the good news. She had been right about Smokey being in one of the machines, he told her, "But he's going to be all right even after thirty-seven days of solitary confinement—without bread and water."

Smokey made a full recovery, and he returned to Dalfonso to go everywhere at her side once again.

5

MEAN AND SCARY CATS

In his book *Possession and Exorcism*, Hans Naegeli-Osjord relates an account of a cat that he suggests might well have been possessed by a demonic entity. According to Naegeli-Osjord, he heard the story in a personal conversation with Dr. Vintila Horia of Madrid.

In Rumania, his country of origin, Horia claimed to have known a woman whose cat urinated on every religious book, even if it was lying underneath other nonreligous texts.

"Once," Horia reported, "the lady wanted to hang up an icon but hammered the nail in crooked. She put the icon on the table and, while looking for a new nail, left the room for a short moment. In her absence, the cat jumped on the table and pawed the icon until it fell and was badly damaged."

The ostensibly antireligious feline also behaved strangely in other ways, and according to its owner was once squarely run over by an automobile without suffering any injury.

Believing that possession is a "unique phenomenon" that is not to be confused with such ego-splitting psychological maladies as clinical schizophrenia, Naegeli-Osjord maintains that even animals may be "infiltrated by the demonic in some way."

While cats tend to be solitary creatures, he notes, they do have close relationships with "significant contact persons." In the bizarre case referred to above, "the demonic . . . may have transferred into the cat" through an association with a possessed human.

The centuries-old ecclesiastical debate over the existence of demonic possession—and the question raised above as to whether or not it can be transferred to animals in general and cats in particular—is not within the province of this book. There are weird cases, however, in which logic simply cannot explain a cat's extremely violent behavior or singular persecution of an individual.

Sheila's Rampage of Terror

To Andrew and Klara Faber, their female gray and white Scottish Fold, called Sheila, was the model of feline propriety and gentleness. They were astonished in March 1990 when they discovered that their neighbors in a suburb of Grand Rapids were about to file a lawsuit against them.

"We knew that Sheila tended to roam while Andy and I were at work," Klara Faber admitted. "But we had no idea of the kind of mischief she was allegedly getting into with our neighbors."

The Fabers' neighbors regarded Sheila's activities as having stretched far beyond mischief. It seemed to them as though the cat were purposefully carrying out an evil vendetta against them.

Henry Gonshak said Sheila not only dug up their plants and vegetables almost as fast as he and his wife, Jean, could plant them, but the ornery cat also invaded their home.

"We would return from work or shopping and find that our sofa pillows had been ripped to shreds," he said. "Our indoor plants would be spilled on the carpet, and it was disgustingly obvious that a cat had used some of the soil for a makeshift litter box. And sometimes it didn't bother with the soil. It left its feces on a sofa cushion."

The Gonshaks confronted the Fabers, but Sheila's owners did not seem to take them seriously.

"Andrew and Klara tried to convince us that we were mistaken," Jean Gonshak said. "It just couldn't be their precious Sheila doing such terrible things. It had to be another cat."

But on the very next day, Henry Gonshak said, when they returned home, "A number of Jean's most valuable collector plates had been dislodged from their places on the wall, and they had been dashed to the floor. We knew that Sheila had paid our home another visit."

Jean Gonshak remembered when Sheila had ruined a family gathering at Christmastime.

"We had invited our children and their families to join us first at church on Christmas morning, then come back to the house for a holiday meal. We found Sheila in our kitchen, contentedly dining on the turkey. Mashed potatoes and pumpkin pies had been splattered all over the floor."

Henry Gonshak said he would happily have torn Sheila limb from limb on that occasion, but the cat seemed literally to disappear before their eyes.

"I don't know how the fiend managed it, but it somehow left the kitchen and got away from us. I went right to the telephone and called the Society for the Prevention of Cruelty to Animals to come and pick up the damned cat; but it being

Christmas and all, there was no one to come out to the neighborhood that day."

Neighbors Leonard and Ellie Murillo also had a complaint to file against the Fabers and Sheila.

"Ellie is extremely allergic to cats," Leonard Murillo said. "And while we like cats, we could never have one for a pet because of her allergy. We could never have one in the house.

"We could not understand it," he continued, "when one night around three in the morning, I had to rush Ellie to the emergency room of the hospital because she could not breathe. It was weird, because I suffer from asthma, and I was having great difficulty breathing as well."

The next afternoon, when Leonard and Ellie had returned home and felt well enough to investigate the mysterious onset of their allergy and asthma attacks, they found cat hairs on Ellie's pillow.

"We looked under the bed and saw balls of white and gray cat fur," Ellie said. "We knew that the Fabers' cat, Sheila, had somehow invaded our home."

Leonard and Ellie began to make it a habit to check their pillows and sheets carefully before retiring. After discovering clumps of cat hair on their pillows and under the bed for three nights in a row, the Murillos followed through on a call to the SPCA.

The fur flew between them and the Fabers when an officer arrived to take Sheila into temporary custody, but the Murillos angrily stood their ground and informed the Fabers in no uncertain terms that they would not tolerate any more uninvited visits from the cat.

"I paid the fine," Andrew Faber said, "but I wanted to know why Leonard and Ellie had done such a thing as to turn Sheila in to the SPCA.

"When they told me about their allergy and asthma attacks and the cat hairs on their bed, I just couldn't believe that our cat could possibly be responsible for such a thing. It seemed ridiculous.

"I asked them how Sheila could have got into their locked house and why she would leave her hair all over and under their bed. I thought they were becoming hysterical when they claimed that Sheila had done it deliberately to make them ill. They actually said they thought our cat was evil."

When the Fabers got word that the Gonshaks were about to file a $50,000 lawsuit against them because of Shelia's hellish raids on their home, Andrew decided to ask a farmer friend to take the cat to the country for a while until things in the neighborhood cooled down.

Andrew's friend returned Sheila after ten days. "Your cat is a monster, pal," he said. "She tore hell out of my cats, nearly blinded our German shepherd, and killed three of our chickens. When we tried to keep her in the house and away from the other farm animals, she ripped our best sofa to shreds."

All this was hard to believe as Klara held the purring Sheila in her arms.

The lawsuit never came to court, but a judge did issue a restraining order to Andrew and Klara to keep their cat indoors or on a leash.

"We agreed to settle with the Gonshaks' insurance companies, because we really do wish to keep peace with our neighbors," Klara Faber said.

"These days, Sheila stays under lock and key in the house or on a thirty-foot leash when she is outside. It is just so hard to imagine that our sweet little Sheila was really responsible for all those terrible things that our neighbors claim."

While Sheila may be an angel to Andrew and Klara, she will always be a demon to the Gonshaks and the Murillos.

Devil Cat Kills Woman after Stalking Her for Three Years

On July 24, 1989, eighty-two-year-old Alicia Ontiveros of Santa Monica, California, was killed by a savage black tomcat that had stalked her for more than three years.

"It was all so absolutely weird and terrible," her daughter, Susana Ferrucci, said. "It was as if Mom were living in a real-life horror movie. For three years she was stalked wherever she went by this big black tomcat. None of us could ever figure out why this cat had it in for her. None of us could ever find out where it had come from."

Ontiveros's brother, Robert, said his sister had asked him whether the family might have had some curse placed on it.

"This cat came from nowhere to attack me and make my life miserable," she said to him. "It has clawed me and bitten me time after time. Why me?"

Robert said he could not provide his sister with a satisfactory answer to this most bizarre of situations.

"Has someone placed a curse on me?" she asked him on more than one occasion. "Or was there some horrible act done to a cat by our family in generations past for which fate has decreed I must pay?"

Robert could only try to reassure her. "Even in the old country where our people were ranchers and farmers," he said, "I have never heard of any of our family mistreating or abusing cats or any other kind of animal."

Ontiveros's son, Arman, confessed that he had doubted his mother's story when the stalking first began in December 1985.

"I thought, Well, Mom is getting up there in years. She has begun to imagine strange things about some stray cat she sees every now and then," he said. "And since she said the cat was black, well, you know, I figured it was just some old superstition.

"I made an awful mistake," Arman said. "I should have listened to my mother. I should not have judged her as being hysterical. Most of all, I should have killed that damn cat!"

Alicia Ontiveros was walking with her next-door neighbor, Nancy Goodwine, when the first attack occurred.

"We were on our way to a nearby market to buy some groceries," Goodwine said. "We always tried to walk together to the grocery store. Anyway, we had hardly walked half a block when this big black cat came flying out of the bushes and landed on Alicia's right arm.

"Alicia and I both screamed in absolute horror. I could tell that Alicia was in awful pain. I hit at the cat with my purse, and Alicia swung her arm back and forth, trying to free herself from the cat's claws and teeth.

"We finally got Alicia away from the monster," Goodwine continued, "but it had left long, deep, bleeding grooves all down the side of her arm. We went back into her house and called a taxi, and I went with her to the doctor to get her bandaged and get her some shots against infection."

From that day on, Alicia Ontiveros became the prey of a relentless hunter. She could not take one step outside her home without the vicious black cat appearing from somewhere—from behind a bush, from the shadows, from her own front steps—to scratch and claw at her.

"How can it always be there whenever I want to leave my

home?" she asked her friends and neighbors. "Does it ever eat or sleep? Does it ever do anything other than lie in wait for me?"

The savage tomcat was not always content to lie in wait for Ontiveros to emerge from her house. On occasion, he tried to claw open a door or window.

"One afternoon when we were having coffee in her kitchen, we heard this terrible growling noise," Goodwine recalled. "We both jumped to our feet, and we were horrified to see the big black cat trying to squeeze itself through this small opening between the window and the sill.

"I grabbed a broom and beat at its head until it withdrew. I was afraid then that the devil cat would begin stalking me, but it never did. It just kept after Alicia."

From that day on, Alicia Ontiveros became a prisoner in her own home. She kept the doors and windows closed and locked even in the hottest weather, and she began to order her groceries over the telephone.

One evening nearly two years after the nightmare had begun, Ontiveros told her daughter, Susana Ferrucci, that she had come to believe that the cat was Satan, tormenting her in feline form.

"I tried to reason with her," Ferrucci said, "but she had it all worked out in her own mind."

Alicia Ontiveros presented a convincing argument that the black cat was a demonic entity.

"Why," she would ask, "would a cat suddenly appear from out of nowhere to persecute me? How can it know always the exact time when I wish to leave my home? What ordinary cat would continue to stalk me for such a long period of time? Yes, it is true. Satan waits for me outside my door."

On many occasions, Robert Ontiveros tried to catch the feline fiend that was tormenting his sister.

"Whenever I came around to put an end to his persecution of Alicia, the beast would be nowhere in sight," he said. "Yet if she would attempt to venture out after I had telephoned from the corner that all was clear, the demon would come spitting, hissing, and scratching at her, seemingly from out of nowhere."

On July 22, 1989, Alicia Ontiveros received word that her dear friend Jeanne Lebeau had died. The funeral service, she was told, would be held on July 24.

"I will attend Jeanne's funeral in spite of the devil cat," she told her neighbor Nancy Goodwine. "The church is only two blocks away, and nothing can stop me from walking there to pay my last respects to a dear old friend."

On July 24, at two o'clock in the afternoon, Alicia Ontiveros opened the door to face her dark nemesis. The scene later reconstructed by the investigating police officers went something like this:

The large black tomcat was sitting on the step, his angry green eyes riveted on the elderly woman. Then, suddenly, the shrieking bundle of fury leaped on her chest, dug his claws firmly into her flesh, and savagely tore her throat open with his fangs.

Ontiveros staggered back inside her home. In a few minutes the life force had spurted out of her.

"We found blood on the steps, on the door, and sprayed throughout the house," a police officer said. "There was blood on the furniture, through the kitchen and hallway ... on the carpets and walls."

Mourning the loss of her friend and shuddering over the horrible nature of her death, Nancy Goodwine sharply criticized Ontiveros's son.

"Arman should have taken his mother seriously when she first told him about that devil cat," she said. "He should have sat outside her house and waited and waited until he had captured that demon from Hell."

According to the police report, a large black tomcat was snared by the animal control officer in the area. It seemed likely that it was the same animal that had terrorized and stalked Ontiveros for three years, and the cat was soon destroyed.

"There are a lot of black cats in the world," Goodwine commented wryly. "Let's hope they destroyed the right one. I would hate to think that spawn of Satan is somewhere out there stalking another elderly victim."

Cat from Hell Terrorizes Oregon Family

"I keep having this terrible nightmare," Becky MacDaniels said. "I hear the doorbell ring, and when I open the door, that godawful cat from Hell is standing there smiling up at me. 'Hi there,' it says. 'I'm back! Want some more?'"

MacDaniels and her two teenage sons, Hugh and Terry, were working in their Washington, Oregon, yard on a peaceful Saturday afternoon in September 1992 when they were attacked by a ferocious stray cat.

"The fiend came at us from out of nowhere," Becky MacDaniels said. "This strange white cat just came bounding at us and started attacking us. Our three dogs were shut up in the house or they might have been able to drive it off. If my husband, Lance, had been home, he probably would have shot the demon and we would have been done with it."

As it was, the devilish cat clawed at their hands and whatever body parts came within its range. Then, hissing and spitting, the vicious creature withdrew to a tree branch.

"But it wasn't retreating," Becky MacDaniels said. "It just wanted a perch where it could dive on us."

Like a maddened Valkyrie swinging its sword and dagger, the cat pounced on Hugh's back and slashed at him with both front paws. Then, while the older boy reeled in pain, the fiend leaped to his younger brother's back and began chewing at the back of his neck.

"By now, I figured the diabolical thing has got to have rabies and has gone berserk," Becky MacDaniels said. "All I can see is that it is chewing on Terry's neck, and I reached out for it with both hands, intending to rip it off and toss it as far as I can. Well, it latched on to me like a chain saw and started ripping my hands and fingers to bloody shreds."

At last the beleaguered MacDaniels family managed to escape the infernal cat's vicious onslaughts and get inside their house.

They called the police, and a few hours later Chief Gordon Simansen had captured the ferocious feline in a skunk trap.

"It was without a doubt the meanest cat I had ever seen," Simansen said. "It snarled at you like a caged panther, and it would try to get at you right through the wires of the cage."

The cat, nicknamed the Terminator by the chief and his men, was taken to the pound for a ten-day rabies observation period.

"If the thing had rabies, then the MacDaniels family were going to be in for more grief; they would have to undergo a painful vaccination process," Simansen said.

But after two days, the fiendish cat escaped from the pound—and somehow found its way back to the MacDaniels' home.

Becky MacDaniels had just returned from the hospital, where she had been receiving treatment for her chewed and mangled hands.

"I had barely walked in the door," she said. "I mean, that

damned diabolical cat almost beat me home. I could not believe it when that fiend out of Hell came running at me in my own kitchen.

"That cat was just plain crazy. It started jumping at the walls, tearing off the wallpaper. How do you figure that?

"Hugh set our three dogs after the monster cat, and it took them all on and nailed them one by one. Two black Labs and a beagle, and it had them all yelping and running for cover.

"After the dogs cleared out, so did the boys and I. Over my shoulder, I could see the cat from Hell going to work on our sofa and stuffed chairs. The kids and I just got the blazes out of the house."

Becky and her sons watched the cat "making a total wreck" of their living room; then the cat began to wind down, as if its vendetta against the MacDaniels family had been somehow satisfied—at least momentarily.

Hugh took advantage of the cat's sudden calm to lure it into an old cage that had once housed a pet rabbit. Terry called Police Chief Simansen with the outlandish news that the cat from Hell had returned to terrorize them.

"This whole incident is one of the weirdest with which I have ever dealt in my twenty-five-year career as a law enforcement officer," Simansen said. "My men and I could hardly believe that the ornery cat had escaped and found its way back to the MacDaniels' home. It really seemed as if that stray cat felt that it had some evil mission to hurt them and to trash their home."

"Thank heavens, our would-be assassin did not have rabies," Becky MacDaniels said. "The report came back from the laboratory negative."

Within a few days, the feline terrorist was destroyed in the pound, its devilish spirit freed to return to whatever nightmare from which it had escaped.

Come Fry with Me

For six years Portia the Parrot and Bunta the Burmese cat had been conducting a running feud that, in retrospect, Scott and Joan Lintelman of Douglas, Nebraska, admit they should have guessed would end in disaster for one of the combatants.

"Portia was my birthday present in 1986," Joan Lintelman said, "and cat and bird took an instant dislike to one another. We had already had Bunta for three years, so I guess he felt he had earned the monopoly on our affections.

"Bunta would stand under Portia's cage and hiss up at her, and Portia would begin the most horrendous squawking whenever she spotted him coming near her."

On one occasion, Bunta knocked the cage stand off-balance and sent Portia—seeds, water dish, toy bell, and all—crashing to the floor.

"It was a good thing we were home, or I'm certain Bunta would have killed Portia at that time," Joan said.

Joan and Scott soundly scolded Bunta, repeating "Bad cat! Bad, bad cat! Bad, bad Bunta!" Portia the parrot immediately mimicked Joan's voice: "Bad, bad cat . . . bad, bad Bunta!"

The feud continued, though limited to hissing and squawking, until that fateful evening in April 1992.

"For whatever reason, Portia was really on Bunta's case that night," Scott said. "She squawked, 'Bad, bad Bunta,' over and over until it was getting on everyone's nerves.

"It finally got to the point where Bunta couldn't handle it, and he was in the process of toppling the cage when I walked into the room and rescued Portia from a nasty fall."

In the midst of a household chore, Scott glanced quickly around and picked out what he thought would be a safer spot for the parrot's cage.

"The top of the stove seemed to me to be a safe place, so I removed the cage from its stand, set it on the stove, and went about my work," Scott said. "By the time I finished, it was bedtime, and I went to sleep without giving Portia and Bunta another thought."

Safe—as she perhaps thought—on the stove, Portia had once again begun the monotonous chant: "Bad, bad cat! Bad, bad Bunta!"

After several hours of the bird's taunts, Bunta jumped up on the counter next to the stove and knocked over a coffee-pot—which fell against a switch and turned on the burner under Portia's plastic-bottomed cage.

Whether it was a freak accident or a demon cat's evil work, within minutes Joan Lintelman's $500 West African parrot had been fried to a crisp.

"We were awakened by the smell of the acrid smoke that was filling the house," Scott said.

"We rushed into the kitchen and saw that Portia was history and that the fire had begun to spread to the counter. We dialed 911 and got out of the house fast . . . and so did Bunta!"

Heartbroken over the loss of her parrot, Joan Lintelman said she should have known that someday the feud between bird and cat would end in a vicious duel to the death.

"I guess Bunta just couldn't take Portia's squawking any longer," she said. "I just wish she hadn't had to die such a terrible death."

At last report, Bunta seemed a much happier cat.

Strange Monster Cats That Haunt the United States

On Monday evening, August 21, 1978, Evelyn Cayton of Belleville, Ohio, was standing on her front porch with some friends. Suddenly everyone present heard strange noises coming from the direction of a demolished chicken coop to the right of the house. Cayton turned on her flashlight, and two pairs of large yellow eyes shone in the beam.

At the same time eighteen-year-old Scott Patterson drove his car toward the coop in hopes of getting a better look with his headlights at whatever was causing the disturbance.

He accomplished his goal: The yellow eyes belonged to what appeared to be two large, black cat-like creatures, which lunged toward Patterson's headlights. All the other witnesses fled into the house.

After the creatures had run off into the night, Patterson immediately telephoned the Stark County sheriff's office, and several deputies were dispatched to investigate the incident. Deputy Sheriff James Shannon reportedly smelled a foul stench in the area of the old chicken coop, and he collected hair samples and made casts of some very strange-looking pawprints.

In the days and weeks that followed, other peculiar catlike creatures and bizarre animal forms were sighted in the region, but all the weird entities escaped from their pursuers unscathed.

Timothy Green Beckley, author of several books on the unknown, has pointed out that throughout the literature of the occult, strange and unusual animal entities have often been associated with demonology, Satanism, and the sinister side of the black arts. Most of these hideous and perverse creatures assume a catlike or a reptilian form.

"These catlike beings that stalk our farms and backwoods do not seem to be flesh and blood in the sense that we consider other living things," Beckley said. "It seems as though it is impossible to trap them; and when they have been shot, they simply disappear in the twinkling of an eye—indicating that they may be more like ghosts than anything else.

"Perhaps there are these catlike creatures that exist in other realms alongside us, who have always been more etheric in content than created of flesh and blood like our own beloved pets."

Even now, as I write this chapter on a November day, I am scanning local newspapers for accounts of the mysterious black cats that have appeared in various parts of Iowa for the past fifty years or so. The frightening felines usually accomplish their first materializations shortly after the early snows have begun to pile up over the clumps of harvested cornstalks and the clods of earth.

Any day, I anticipate, some farmer will spot one of the dark creatures—stark against the white drifts—crouching near his mailbox at the end of the lane. Or maybe the phantom cat will be bothering his chickens.

I remember clearly the winter of 1971, when a strange catlike creature was sighted in northeastern Iowa. Whatever the thing was, it proved to have an enormous appetite: It ate large sections of several pigs. Perhaps in self-defense—or maybe just for sport—it broke the necks of a number of large dogs.

I will be disappointed if there aren't at least a few accounts of ghostly black felines in the approaching winter months. The monster cats have been haunting Iowans intermittently ever since I can remember; and now that my wife, Sherry, and I have just returned to Iowa after fifteen years in the deserts of Arizona, I will take it personally if they don't rematerialize.

Year after year, in nearly every section of the United States, sensible men and women file reports of large, catlike monsters marauding about the landscape. A particularly strange aspect of their raids on farms and ranches is that these cat creatures are never shot or killed—even though they are widely and earnestly hunted by experienced woodsmen.

This is not because the weird beasties don't have tracks; in fact, they make catlike pawprints all over—pawprints which can never be precisely identified, but which beyond doubt are not those of any known indigenous animal.

On a fall evening in 1968, a Connecticut Company bus driver swore he had seen something that looked like a baby tiger or a huge tabby cat walk across a street and disappear into the brush. He told police officers he had made the sighting about five P.M. near West Rock.

Although seven New Haven police cruisers were on the scene within minutes of the call, they could find no creature that resembled a monster cat in the area.

At about the same time in Branford, Connecticut, a large "cat-creature" was seen walking in "an almost stately way" near the driveway of Senator Lucy T. Hammer's forty-acre country estate.

The senator's husband had first sighted the great catlike animal strutting near their driveway. Thorvald Hammer, an iron company executive, had been eating breakfast when he spotted the bizarre intruder.

The tracking dogs of game wardens and police found only the slashed remains of a squirrel.

Later, in her comments to journalists, Senator Hammer said

106   *Brad Steiger*

her husband had left the house and his breakfast and had watched the mysterious animal walking in a "most stately manner down our path." Thorvald Hammer had lost sight of the creature when it went around a bend.

"The strange animal must have gone into the woods," the senator concluded.

Or did the cat-creature walk around the bend and reenter the other dimension of time and space from which it had briefly emerged?

Whenever farmers and ranchers in Iowa, South Dakota, Nebraska, or Ohio complain that a monstrous cat has been mangling their livestock, it is easy enough to theorize that a cougar has migrated from a more westerly state in search of better hunting grounds. The trouble is, none of the physical traces ever seem to be the sort left by a nomadic cougar, puma, mountain lion, or panther (they're all different names for the same big cat, depending on which section of the country you hail from).

In May and June 1959 (to choose one of hundreds of reports), residents of the western section of Lorain County, Ohio, were having problems with a giant catlike beast possessed of a large head, a huge, light brown body, and an insatiable appetite for dogs, cats, and sheep.

Iva Witteman of Royalton Road in Columbia Station went out to check her eight sheep at about eight P.M. She found six of them ripped apart. One had been completely skinned, and the eighth was missing.

A sheriff's deputy said he had never seen anything like it. He ruled out a dog pack. Iva Witteman, her husband, and a friend had been visiting in the Wittemans' house only 250 yards from the pasture in which the sheep were kept, and they had heard nothing.

In July 1964, the tales of cat-creatures featured a five-foot-tall, tailless, earless, 200-pound feline that walked on its hind legs.

Two campers on Mount Tamalpais in Marin County, California, complained to authorities that two such entities had disturbed them on three occasions. They reported that the "cat-people" had heads close to their bodies and were very muscular below the shoulders. In one instance, the two campers had heard the creatures "chittering" back and forth for about seven hours.

Also in 1964, Samuel Johnson, a Chicago motorist, confronted his worst cat-monster nightmare on a road near Niles, Michigan. He could remember it only as "something that had red eyes, brown hair, and squealed." Johnson's car window had been shattered in four places where he said the creature had struck it.

On April 10, 1970, Mike Busby of Cairo, Illinois, was traveling on Route 3 to Olive Branch to pick up his wife.

About a mile south of Olive Branch on the dark, deserted road that parallels the edge of Shawnee National Forest, Busby's car broke down. Grumbling, Busby got out and popped open the hood.

He had not even had time to glance at the motor when he was distracted by a noise to his left. Without warning, a catlike form about six feet tall moved in on him and hit him in the face. Busby and his monstrous attacker fell together to the highway. Dull claws ripped at his clothing, and Busby sought with all his strength to hold the thing's mouth open and at arm's length so that its awful teeth could not tear his throat.

Although he could not see clearly what it was that had seized him, Busby said later he could feel something fuzzy around its mouth and that the thing's body hair was short and wiry, like steel wool.

The cat-creature kept emitting deep, soft growls—"sounds unlike anything I had ever heard," Busby said.

After what must have seemed like an eternity, a diesel truck approached with bright headlights and the roar of a powerful motor—which appeared to frighten Busby's attacker back into the forest.

Spotlighted for a moment in the headlights, the creature appeared to be "a sleek, shiny black color." Busby also noted that it ran away on heavy, thudding feet.

John Hartsworth, the truck driver, said the thing he saw in his headlamps looked like some kind of "giant cat" until it raised itself off Busby and ran into the forest on its hind legs.

If you're ready to conclude that we humans are being stalked by vicious cat-creatures from the undiscovered planet Felix, consider the following account:

When six-year-old Debbie Dierking disappeared from her home in northern Michigan about six P.M. on August 15, 1988, local and state police, a crew of volunteers, and two police bloodhounds scoured a four-mile wooded area.

The Dierking family was in shock. There was no note, so kidnapping was ruled out; at any rate, the Dierkings' modest neighborhood and six-year-old Chevrolet in the driveway ought to have discouraged any hopes of a large ransom.

Of course, the Dierking household had been carefully searched before the original alarm about Debbie's absence had been issued. In addition, a deputy police chief and the rector of the Roman Catholic church the Dierkings attended had also explored the house three times.

Even so, Debbie was found before dawn the next morning, peacefully sleeping on her own bed.

When her gratefully weeping stunned parents asked Debbie where she had been, she stubbornly refused to tell them.

Stern police officers, solicitous neighbors, and coaxing relatives all got the same answer: "I'm not telling!"

Investigators wondered whether some crazed kidnapper had thought better of a dangerous and unprofitable gambit and had returned the child, desperately making a game of it all with Debbie and forcing her to promise she would not tell where she had been—or with whom.

Several days later, though, the girl at last confided in her mother that she had been found in the forest and safely returned to her bed by a "cat guy" who looked like "the nice lion man" on the *Beauty and the Beast* television show. "You know,"—Debbie smiled and crinkled her nose—"the nice cat man with the cape who lives in the sewer and saves the pretty lady."

If Debbie's account can be believed, some cat-like entity— or perhaps some person disguised with cat-creature makeup similar to that donned by actor Ron Perlman in the television series—rescued her and escorted her safely home.

Is it possible that some cosmic, interdimensional being with catlike features and feline shape removed the child for a time for some unfathomable purpose of its own, then brought her back to her own plane with the promise not to betray its secret?

If another, unknown dimension somehow shares this planet with our own three-dimensional reality, it may be safe to assume that it is inhabited by an intelligent species of some kind which shares its world with assorted animals, birds, reptiles, and fish. And if it is possible that from time to time "holes" or "doorways" appear in our dimension or theirs which permit passage between the two worlds, it may be that all the creatures of our legends, myths, and nightmares have their origin on this other plane of reality.

Bizarre Superstitions and Beliefs about Cats

Perhaps no animal inspires such devotion and dedication—
and such animosity and abhorrence—as the cat. Throughout
history, cats have been regarded as gods by certain cultures
and as demons by others. With such a centuries-old mystique
swirling around the figure of the cat, it's no wonder that those
silent little paws have left heavy imprints in the collective
psyches of those who love them, those who revere them, and
those who fear them.

According to Jewish tradition, God had no hand in the making of cats. The first female and male cat couple were snorted
from the nostrils of a lion as it was boarding Noah's Ark.

In European tradition, the black cat is the familiar companion of witches. The Inquisitors with their awful instruments
of torture decreed that all cats were demons and condemned
nearly as many cats to the stake as witches.

It is because of this baseless old ecclesiastical judgment that
the sighting of a black cat is said to be an omen of misfortune,
and that unhappiness and personal tragedy will soon follow
in the wake of the black cat that crosses one's path.

The great British novelist Charles Dickens, who was fasci-
nated by tales of the supernatural and the macabre, spoke in

his later years of stories his nursemaid had told him that caused him nightmares and cold sweats. One of them was about the Black Cat; in his *The Uncommercial Traveller*, Dickens remembered that the grim tale was about "a weird and glowing-eyed supernatural Tom, who was reputed to prowl about the world by night, sucking the breath of infancy, and who was endowed with a special thirst (as I was given to understand) for mine."

Of all the animals over which humans convince themselves that they hold dominion, the cat is the only one that looks us in the eye with a steady gaze that scorns subservience and assures us that the cat possesses magical powers, whether for good or for evil.

Some people believe that the unwavering stare of the cat can instill terror, even cause death. Such an unreasoning, fearful response to cats is known as ailurophobia. Hitler had plans to dominate the world with his Third Reich, but the sight of a cat set him trembling. Napoleon Bonaparte arrogantly snatched the crown of the Holy Roman Emperor from the Pope and conquered nearly all Europe, but when he spotted a cat in his palace, he shouted for help.

Such dread of cats may be genetically transmitted; when Joseph Bonaparte, King of Naples, visited Saratoga Springs in 1825, he complained just before he fainted that he sensed a cat's presence. Although his hosts assured His Majesty that no such animal was anywhere present, a persistent search revealed a kitten hiding in a sideboard.

Henry III of England was another personage of royal blood who would faint at the sight of a cat.

Besides a glance that can bring on terror, folklore also empowers the cat's eyes with the ability to see in the dark. Since all other creatures can see only in the daylight, to see at night reverses the natural order of things and is perceived as sinister and Satanic.

In the Middle Ages, the brain of a black cat was an essential ingredient in all powerful potions.

An ancient superstition has it that spirits can assume the forms of black animals, particular black cats. This belief only enhanced the cat's reputation as a harbinger of ill fortune. Women who believed themselves to be witches sought cats, which might be possessed by spirits, to serve as their familiars and do their bidding.

An old black-letter book titled *Beware the Cat!* (1584) warns that black cats may be witches in disguise. One might kill a black cat, believing that one has killed the witch, but the brutal act does not necessarily guarantee the elimination of this servant of the devil—for a witch can assume the body of a cat nine times.

During the terrible witchcraft trials of the Inquisition, heretics under torture confessed to kissing cats' buttocks and toads' mouths and cavorting with them in blasphemous ceremonies. Some poor wretches claimed that Satan first appeared to them in the form of a cat, for it was commonly held that cats were allied with Lucifer in the great rebellion against God. Lucifer, so the counter-gospel proclaimed, was the true Creator, and one day he would lead his followers back to Heaven to cast the ursurper deity from the throne of glory.

It seems likely that the contemporary passion for cats began in ancient Egypt, where the first domesticated cats descended from a wild ancestor called *felis libyca* The Egyptians not only did not fear the black cat, but they reverenced it. A cemetery containing the mummies of thousands of black cats was unearthed in Egypt, and a cargo of the mummified felines was sent to Great Britain.

The folk belief that a cat possesses nine lives goes back to the inhabitants of those ancient cities on the Nile. Bast (or

Ubasti), the Cat-Mother goddess, was associated with the benevolent aspect of Hathor, the Lioness, and was said to have nine lives. The peculiar attribute of Bast's nine incarnations became linked in the common mind with all cats.

The Egyptians elevated cats far above the role of domestic pet. To the Egyptians, the cat was transformed from mouse catcher to supreme deity, the "Sayer of Great Words." The Egyptian word for cat was *Mau*, which is at once an imitation of the animal's call and the nearly-universal human cry for mother. Cats came to be worshipped with such intensity that the wanton killing of a cat was punishable by death.

Because the old Egyptians had a great fear of the dark, they observed with awe that the cat, a creature of the night, walked the shadowed streets with confidence. Carefully considering the import of the cat's midnight vigils, the Egyptian sages decided that the cat was solely responsible for preventing the world from falling into eternal darkness.

At the same time, the cat's nocturnal excursions made it a symbol of sexuality and fertility. It seems quite likely that long before Cleopatra worked her magic on Caesar and Antony, the sirens of the Nile used makeup that mimicked the hypnotic eyes and facial markings of the cat.

Bubastis, a city in Lower Egypt, dedicated itself to the worship of the cat. Each May some 700,000 pilgrims journeyed to the city to participate in a cat festival.

During the Persian invasion of 529 B.C., the Egyptians' idealization of the cat proved their undoing. Knowing of the obsession of the Egyptian people with the divinity of felines, Cambyses II, King of the Persians, made a cat part of the standard issue to each of his soldiers. The Nile-dwellers led by King Psamtik III laid down their spears and bows for fear of harming the cat each soldier carried, and the Persians conquered the city of Pelusium without shedding a drop of blood.

The cat was also held sacred in ancient India. Sanskrit writings make numerous references to the influence of the cat on humankind.

In Scandinavian countries, girls used to try their best to be married on a Friday, Freya's day. Freya, often depicted being drawn in a chariot by two cats, is the cat-goddess of the Nordic people. If a young woman married on a sunny Friday, it was known that she had taken good care of the family cats and that Freya would bless the union.

The Voodoo Priest "Put Puss" on Him

In the book *True Experiences in Exotic ESP*, edited by Martin Ebon, Grace N. Isaacs contributes a chapter titled "Psychic Animals of the Caribbean" in which she describes how a modern-day practitioner of the dark arts set a familiar spirit in the form of a cat on a Christian clergyman.

It seems that the Reverend Mr. R., an Australian who resided in Jamaica *circa* 1916, took a member of his congregation to task for continuing to visit the *obeah* man, the local Voodoo priest. The fellow who had received such a firm chastisement from the minister did not respond in at all a penitent manner. He went straight to the *obeah* man and repeated the minister's scolding word for word. The Voodoo priest believed that the Australian interloper had overstepped the bounds of ecumenical tolerance, and he sent word to Reverend R. that he had put "puss 'pon him."

As might be expected, the orthodox clergyman was amused by this information. He told the *obeah* man's messenger that never in his life had he been frightened by nonsensical threats, and that "puss or no puss," he would continue to perform his clerical duties as he saw fit.

A short time after having so summarily dismissed the Voodoo priest's messenger, however, the Reverend R. was forced to observe that he seldom walked the streets of the village without a cat following at his heels.

According to Isaacs, "If he visited friends or a member of the congregation, a cat would jump on the arm of his chair. On the last occasion before the nuisance abated, he preached for a minister in another parish, and a cat found its way to the pulpit and perched itself in the spot where the minister would have placed his notes. It refused to be driven away, and the verger at last had to remove it bodily."

6

EERIE GHOST CATS

Josh McCarthy, an elderly blind man in Milwaukee, was nearly inconsolable when his beloved Burmese cat died of old age in 1985.

"Dad had lived with us for about eight years," said Esther Kelly, his youngest daughter. "Old Oscar had kept Dad company for so many years."

"Dad would sit for hours in his old rocking chair, stroking Oscar and telling stories to the kids about his life on the railroad. I didn't figure Dad would last long after Oscar died."

Then one afternoon, Josh summoned his daughter to his side.

"Dad was crying and smiling at the same time," Esther Kelly said.

" 'Listen! Listen!' he said. 'Old Oscar has come back to me.' "

Kelly bent her head toward his lap as her father motioned for her to do. "Oscar had this funny, weird, raspy kind of purr," she said. "And I could hear that old cat's familiar purring."

When she stepped back, she could see the indentation of

a weight on her father's lap. "Dad was stroking an invisible cat, and he was happy again.

"Some mean-spirited folks might say that Dad is crazy—lost his mind when his old cat died. But I have heard that ghost cat purr, and I believe it is there on his lap once again.

"I guess Oscar's return has proved to our whole family that love can open a big door between life and death."

Dr. T. J. Muckle of Kingston, Ontario, watched in amazement as the ghost of his beloved cat manifested itself before his eyes. The Canadian physician was sitting in his living room in the afternoon when he saw the family tabby floating slowly across the room. The remarkable tale of the floating ghost cat is recounted in John Robert Colombo's book, *Mackenzie King's Ghost, Plus 49 Other Canadian Hauntings*.

Continuing the account, Muckle said, "Our cat, Tom, walked past me in midair, and he seemed completely real and alive except that he was floating. I was absolutely shocked and baffled.

"Sadly, I found out later that our cat had been run over by a car miles away at that precise moment.

"A neighbor who witnessed the accident phoned. But by then, our dead cat had already come over to say goodbye to us, and perhaps to let us know he still loved us."

Timothy Green Beckley of Inner Light Publishing Company in New York recalled his acquaintance with a ghost cat, the spirit of a favorite pet that apparently survived physical death.

"When I was in my early teens, my family had a very frisky cat named Sweety who had silver-gray hair and beautiful green eyes," Beckley said. "Sweety would hide in all sorts of places in the house and yard.

"Yet whenever he heard the tinkling of a little bell that we kept near his food and water dish, he would come running at full speed. It was a funny sight to see him trying to scamper across a newly waxed floor, his legs moving rapidly—but his furry body standing still due to the slippery linoleum surface."

Sweety lived to a ripe old age, Beckley recalled, and the family was heartbroken when their lively feline friend finally passed away.

"Many years later," he said, "my father still lived in the same house. Since my sister and her family have a place of their own nearby, they were able to visit Pops more frequently than I was able to do. On several occasions, my sister Bobby-jane swore that she saw Sweety run by her as if he were on his way to eat."

Bobbyjane insisted that she saw the ghost of their favorite pet many times. "In fact, I've almost tripped over Sweety," she said. "He just zips right through the kitchen and then disappears."

Beckley said his sister's testimony has been corroborated.

"My nephew Brian has said that he has seen a cat on the stairs leading to the grandmother's apartment. Although he has tried to catch the animal many times, the cat vanishes before his eyes."

Beckley pointed out that Brian is much too young to have seen Sweety in real life. "The cat died many years before he was born. Yet Brian's description of the ghost cat with the silver-gray hair and the beautiful green eyes is so similar as to be nerve-rattling."

Since Timothy Green Beckley's publishing company special-izes in books about UFOs, ESP, ghosts, prophecy, and magic, he is considered an authority on the strange and the bizarre and is a frequent guest on radio and television talk shows.

Beckley recalled a time a few years back when he was ap-pearing on *The Dennis Benson Show*, broadcast over WDVE radio in Pittsburgh, and learned that his family home was not unique in its possession of a ghost cat.

Around eight A.M., a listener telephoned with the following story:

"I've got this huge German shepherd who is very playful. He used to run all over the house chasing my pet alley cat, Alex.

"Recently Alex got hit by a car and died. When the cat didn't show up around the house anymore, the German shepherd acted like he had lost his best friend. He really had the blues.

"Then one day I heard two sets of paws running back and forth in the hallway. I looked out my bedroom door, and there was my dog chasing *something* down the hall. A few feet in front of the German shepherd, I could see the dim outline of Alex—transparent, but still visible just the same.

"The cat went right through the wall, and my poor dog nearly killed himself because he wasn't able to stop soon enough."

The listener concluded his account by saying that Alex the ghostly cat had shown up four or five times after that initial appearance. He added that the German shepherd seemed happy to have his old friend back.

Seventy-seven-year-old Sarah Devietro was terribly distressed when she heard the news about Bucky in September 1982. In tears she told her husband, Tony, that the beloved cat they had given to friends had been put to death.

"We only gave Bucky up because we thought we were getting too old to care properly for him," she said.

"Cissie and Dave had to put Bucky to sleep because the rules of their new apartment house in Miami forbade them to keep pets. Why, oh, why, did they not call us and ask us to take Bucky back?"

Tony was also very upset. They had both loved the tomcat, himself nearly fifteen years old. They would gladly have taken back their old feline friend.

According to the Devietros, they first heard the scratching at their bedroom door about a week after they had learned the sad news of Bucky's execution. The noises became so insistent and so loud that they were both awakened from a sound sleep.

"By all the saints," Sarah said, "Tony and I saw our bedroom door swing open. We keep a little night-light on, so we could clearly see that nothing visible had entered our room. The door had been opened by an unseen force."

Then, to their astonishment and delight, the elderly couple felt something jump on their bed—and they *felt* Bucky bouncing across the covers the way he had always moved in life. Tears came to their eyes as they clearly heard affectionate purring fill the room.

"People can call us old fools if they like," Tony said. "But we have a real ghost cat in our home. We know it is Bucky, and he jumps up on our bed nearly every night."

Sarah said she could sometimes feel the invisible cat rubbing up against her legs. "A couple of times we even found cat hairs on the sofa pillow in the living room. That spot used to be Bucky's favorite to sneak up and take a nap."

The most important thing Bucky's ghostly return demonstrates to Sarah and Tony is that their cat did not blame them for his untimely death.

"His coming back lets us know that he still loves us," Tony said, "and that love between animals and humans can reach across the grave. Sarah and I will probably be ghosts ourselves one day soon. Bucky has gone on ahead to find a home for us."

Music teacher Ruth Wharton, who now resides in La Jolla, California, once owned a white part-Siamese cat named Snooky that she loved very much.

"Snooky used to sit outside the door to the house and wait for my music pupils to arrive for a lesson," Wharton said. "By positioning himself right beside the door, he would be certain to be petted by each of the pupils before they entered."

Wharton announced her firm conviction that Snooky was psychic. "He would play and meow to unknown spirit cats that I could not see.

"Snooky could also tell when my husband would come down the street in his car. Wherever he might be, Snooky would come running as fast as he could to welcome my husband home."

One day after his regular feeding time, Snooky did not return.

Wharton said she searched everywhere, calling his name over and over. "But Snooky never came home again."

One month from the day that he disappeared, Snooky's ghostly image appeared in the tree outside Wharton's window.

"I was in the middle of giving a piano lesson when suddenly the pupils turned toward the window—and there on a branch in the tree was Snooky," Wharton said. "It was really my cat, and he went up on the roof and began to meow. I went out on the patio with my pupils and called him, but we never heard him again."

On two other occasions, however, Snooky did return in a similar manner to inform his owner that he was alive and well—just in a different form.

"Such experiences have convinced me that no one ever dies," Wharton said, "whether you are a human or an animal."

Gabriel's Protective Gaze Circumvents Death

Twilight was just beginning to lengthen the shadows in the northern Minnesota forest on that day in November 1967. Craig Russell was hiking back to his pickup truck after a day of hunting when he sensed something stirring in the brush.

"I was disgusted to see that someone had shot a young tomcat, the kind that we used to call New England barn cats, a big gray striped cat," Russell said.

"I knew a lot of hunters and conservation officers routinely shot cats that were straying into hunting areas. I understood why one might decide a cat had no business trespassing, but I could not forgive the carelessness of a hunter who would not be certain of his target and leave an animal to die a lingering death."

Russell pointed his shotgun at the dying cat. "I would at least put him out of his misery. He had been shot in the throat, and whenever he tried to make a sound, bubbles of blood formed and burst around the hole in his neck."

Russell's finger tightened around the trigger. "But then I looked into his eyes and it seemed as though I received some kind of telepathic request for mercy. I put the shotgun on safety, leaned it against a nearby tree trunk, and bent down to take a closer look at the wounded tom.

"Upon a more complete examination, I made a layman's assessment that the cat might have used up a couple of its nine lives, but with a little human care, it would probably live. The bullet, small-caliber, perhaps a twenty-two, had passed completely through his throat without causing a great deal of damage—other than setting free a lot of blood."

Not truly understanding why, Russell picked up the tomcat, carried him back to his pickup, and brought home a bloody, furry surprise to Donna, his wife.

Within a week, the Russells had the young tom up on his feet and eating hearty meals.

The only permanent injury was to the cat's voice. One night he began to meow for the first time since Craig Russell had brought him home, and both of the Russells started laughing at the bizarre sound the cat produced.

"He honks like a Canadian goose!" Donna said.

"He sounds like a very bad trumpet player," Craig said. "I hope when Gabriel the archangel appears on Judgment Day, his trumpet sounds better than that."

The Russells burst into renewed laughter as they realized they had just discovered their pet's name: Gabriel.

Gabriel did not seem resentful that his peculiar honking meow always amused the Russells and their guests. The tomcat just seemed happy to have found a home, and he spent every evening curled up beside Craig's chair, as if keeping a watchful eye over the human being who had saved his life.

"He seemed to love watching me work," Craig said. "I had begun writing some free-lance articles on outdoor life and hunting. I had been having some luck selling a few pieces, and I would sit every night after I had finished working at my 'real' job at the supermarket and bang away at the typewriter. Gabriel would sit and watch me strike those keys by the hour."

Gabriel maintained his protective gaze for more than thirteen years. Then one night in July 1980, the tomcat just kept looking at Craig when his master made repeated calls for bedtime.

"Gabriel died a very peaceful and gentle death," Craig Russell said. "Those loving eyes just kept staring at me without blinking after I called him and called him to come to bed. Finally I knelt down beside him and found that he had died while watching me finish another article for a wildlife magazine."

Two years later, Craig Russell received his first big, all-expenses-paid assignment from a popular sports magazine. He was to travel to a newly opened resort in a northeastern state and write a review of the facilities. He was warned that conditions would be a bit rustic, but life in northern Minnesota had equipped him for the wild.

The resort sought to capture the flavor of an early 1900s hunting lodge, and Russell believed the effect they had achieved was authentic and ruggedly charming. He would spend the next day hiking the woods around the resort.

"I fell into a dead sleep," he said. "I had put in a very full, and rather strenuous, day. But I was awakened in the middle of the night by Gabriel's unmistakable honking trumpet blasts. At first my dream mechanism fit the sounds into a wonderful dream scenario that Gabriel was not dead and that he was with me.

"Then I sat bolt upright in bed, remembering where I was. Once again, I clearly heard Gabriel's 'horn' honking away at me to get up."

Russell pulled on his trousers, flipped on his boots, and opened the door to discover the hall outside his room filled with smoke. He had barely exited the hallway when a sudden draft from somewhere in the lodge ignited the area with an explosive blast.

"My room had become a tinderbox. I couldn't even step back into it to get my suitcase or my clothes. Fortunately, I had on my trousers and boots, and someone handed me a coat," Russell said.

"Everyone thought it was a miracle that I had awakened in time to escape the fire. The men on either side of me had not been so fortunate."

While a rural fire department worked to save the remainder of the lodge, Russell stood quietly looking up at the moon, tears coursing freely down his cheeks. He knew his old friend Gabriel was still watching over him.

Blue Angel Battles Evil Ghost Cat to Save Owners' Baby Boy

A few years ago, a young couple of my acquaintance rented an old house in a medium-sized city in Wisconsin before moving to their new split-level home. For several nights after they had moved into the old house, their two-year-old daughter awakened with screams of terror.

The solicitous mother carefully examined her daughter, trying to determine exactly what could cause the child such anxiety. After a week, the girl refused to sleep in her own room, and her parents were forced to move her into their bedroom for the four months they remained in the house.

"There *was* something about that one particular room," the father told me. "After I took the time to investigate a bit, I could definitely understand why Jennifer refused to sleep in there. At night when I was getting ready for bed, I found

myself glancing toward that door, as if I expected someone—
or *something*—to come walking out."

The mother confided that she had once felt something
brush across her ankles when she was in the room. She described the sensation as feeling very much as though an invisible cat were brushing against her ankles.

Although such a sensation might be pleasant under ordinary
circumstances, she said it had filled her "with absolute loath-
ing, as if some repulsive creature had reached out and touched
me."

It was not until the young family had moved into their
new home that they learned that an elderly recluse and his
three aging Siamese cats had once lived in the old house.
According to the story they were told, the recluse had first
poisoned his cats, then hanged himself in the bedroom they
had used for their daughter's nursery. Several previous tenants
had also complained of "something odd" being centered in
that particular room.

As eerie as their experience may have been, my young
friends' encounter with a ghostly cat pales in comparison with
an account of an evil phantom feline given to me by Henry
and Carol Salvato of Houston.

In May 1975, the Salvatos acquired the key to a house that
seemed to have been built just for them. Both Henry and
Carol believed it was a stroke of good fortune that had delivered the magnificent old home in the Houston suburb into
their hands. They never doubted they and their children, seven-
year-old Sandi and eleven-month-old Steven, would be happy
and secure in their new home. There was also a spacious yard
for Blue Angel, their four-year-old Russian Blue cat, to romp
and climb trees in.

But as pleasant as the house had initially appeared and as
lovingly as the Salvatos had furnished it, after the first three
or four days, both Henry and Carol became sensitive to an

air of foreboding that seemed to hang over the place. And neither of them could ignore Blue Angel's strange behavior in certain rooms. Once the cat had arched his back and growled at something invisible to them.

Hoping to dispel the gloomy atmosphere, they telephoned Father Martin Thalheimer to deliver a traditional blessing on the house.

The priest, a man in his mid-fifties, seemed cheery enough until he paused in the hallway outside a spare upstairs bedroom. "Something gave me a bit of chill there," he said, smiling apologetically. "I'm glad ... very pleased that you asked me to give the blessing to your new home."

On the first weekend they spent in the house, the Salvatos were awakened by a slamming door.

Henry and Carol sat upright, Carol reaching out instinctively to protect the baby, who slept between them. They listened in the darkness, and from somewhere in the house they again heard the sound of a slamming door.

Henry told his wife a door must be caught in the wind. To himself, he wondered whether the wind could turn the knob on a latch door, then open and close it.

He slipped out of bed to investigate. Although a man of uncommon courage, with a distinguished record in Vietnam, Henry later admitted that the eerie sounds not only bewildered him, but made him feel uneasy.

As he stood in the kitchen, he heard a series of scratching sounds, which seemed to him very much like the noise a scrambling animal would make as it scurried for cover.

Blue Angel stood fast beside him, glancing quizzically about the room, his vivid green eyes seeking to penetrate the mystery of the strange sounds.

"I don't see anything, either, buddy," Henry said to his cat. "Where are those noises coming from? And what the hell is making them?"

Blue Angel answered with a low, throaty growl that startled Henry. The cat was normally quiet, almost shy. It was completely out of the ordinary to hear him growl.

At the sound of Blue Angel's warning, the noises in the kitchen suddenly stopped.

The silence itself seemed a prelude to something even more bizarre and unsettling, but Henry smiled and said, "Hey, boy, you scared off whatever it was!"

A thud sounded from the ceiling above them as if in contemptuous response; then all was silent once again.

From that evening on, the Salvatos were visited nightly by an array of sounds. The greatest concentration came about midnight, and no matter how tightly the doors had been secured, they banged to and fro as if they had a will of their own. Eerie whispers of half-words and snatches of nearly understandable phrases echoed in the air around them whenever they went to investigate.

Both Henry and Carol were coming to believe that these nocturnal manifestations could have no natural explanation, and they began to understand why the magnificent house had stood empty for so long and why its price had been so low. Their dream home was beginning to transform itself into a nightmare.

"We could see that Blue Angel's sensitivity made him very susceptible to the phenomena," Carol said. "He would arch his back and hiss and spit whenever he walked into the bedroom above the kitchen, which was where the manifestations seemed most concentrated. We were thankful that Sandi appeared unaffected by the haunting—or at least we thought she was."

One afternoon while Carol was straightening her daughter's room, she found a number of long white cat hairs on the bed. The hairs were not Blue Angel's.

When she asked Sandi whether she knew anything about the strange hairs, the child's answer made her shiver.

"I guess they must be from the big white kitty that comes and sits on my bed every night, Mommy. Blue Angel is terribly jealous of her, and he always chases her away whenever she comes to play with me."

When the Salvatos heard about the white ghost cat that was materializing on their daughter's bed they decided Sandi would begin sleeping in their room.

"Thank God we had not put her in the bedroom where the greatest concentration of supernatural power occurred," Carol said. "We almost did make that Sandi's room because it was so bright and sunny during the day. But one evening when we had come back to inspect the house just before we moved in, it had felt so gloomy and oppressive."

Loud, unexplained bumps and thumps issued from the haunted bedroom every night, but after the third week of the Salvatos' occupancy, they also began to happen occasionally during the day—and in other areas of the house.

Once when Carol was cleaning the kitchen, she felt a cold draft and what she described as "icy fingertips" running over her body. At almost the same moment, she felt what she at first thought was Blue Angel rubbing himself against her ankle.

"I distinctly felt something soft and furry rubbing against my leg, and when I saw that it was not Blue Angel and remembered that he was upstairs with Sandi, my whole body began to shake with fear and revulsion," she said.

Carol Salvato told herself resolutely that if she refused to fear such manifestations, they could do her no harm.

Henry reasoned nearly the same way. An evil presence clearly resided in the house, but both were certain that fear of it would only give it greater power over them. Both had been raised as Roman Catholics, and they considered themselves religious and spiritual people.

"Carol and I told ourselves that only those who feared supernatural forces could be harmed by them," Henry said. "We firmly believed that to be a reasonable assumption."

One hot night in early June, the Salvatos were awakened by Steven's crying out between them on the bed. Blue Angel appeared to have been disturbing the baby, and Henry snatched up the cat quite roughly.

He was in the process of removing Blue Angel from the room when Sandi cried out that their cat friend had just saved Baby Stevie.

"The big white cat was sitting on Stevie's face!" Sandi said, beginning to cry. "It was trying to hurt the baby. The white cat is not nice. It let me play with it, but it is not nice. It wanted to hurt our baby! Blue Angel jumped up on your bed and chased the bad cat away."

Carol nearly became hysterical at the thought that their son could have died from supernatural suffocation. Both she and Henry were horrified at the notion that whatever evil presence infected the house had been bold enough to materialize between them, attempting to claim the life of their child.

"We've got to call Father Thalheimer in the morning," Henry said. "We must ask him to perform an exorcism and rid this house of whatever evil lives here."

The next evening, after the rite of exorcism was completed, Father Thalheimer crossed himself, then addressed the Salvatos.

"The ceremony to purge has been performed," he said softly. A worried look came over his face, and he added, "The performance of the rite, however, is no guarantee that the spirits will not return."

At that instant a tapping sounded from the ceiling. Carol looked up in fear before falling into the arms of her husband, whose face was set in an expression of grim determination.

When the tapping had ceased, Father Thalheimer continued speaking. "I would have called you had you not summoned me. I have recently completed some inquiries about the history of this house, and I must inform you that there is evil here."

According to the priest, the previous owners had moved out of the house after the tragic death of their baby by mysterious suffocation.

"The child had been in perfect health," Father Thalheimer continued. "The child's death occurred on a warm night in June, and the family had used no bedcovers. There were no marks of any kind on the infant, yet it died of apparent suffocation."

Henry felt his wife's hands gripping his arms. Carol was trembling.

"Like yourselves," the priest said, "the previous occupants of this house and certain of their visitors had reported seeing the manifestation of a large, white cat."

Carol could no longer repress her tears. "If it had not been for Blue Angel," she said, "our baby might have been suffocated last night as he slept between us."

"There is more," the priest said. His voice grew unsteady. "The original owners of this house were said to have been practitioners of the dark arts. After they appeared to have died in some kind of ritual suicide, it came out that during the course of their evil practices they had abused several children from the area. The death of their own infant son may actually have been a sacrifice to Satan rather than an accident, as it had been officially decreed. Both of the Satanists had dyed their hair white and had a number of white cats that they appear to have sacrificed on a regular basis."

Carol Salvato looked pale. "Why weren't we given any of the history of this place before we moved in?"

"That's obvious!" Henry replied with a derisive burst of laughter. "Who in their right mind would buy such a place?"

"Leave this unholy house!" Father Thalheimer said. "Take your children and leave at once."

Henry shook his head. "It's just not that easy. We put every cent we had into this house. We couldn't afford another until this one sold. And that"—he laughed wryly—"probably won't happen again in our lifetime! No one wants to buy a house that kills kids!"

Henry looked at his wife, then at the priest. "No," he said resolutely, "we will not be driven from our house by nasty spirits. We cannot allow whatever infects this house to defeat us. We can't!"

As if in retort, the unexplainable tapping began once again on the kitchen ceiling.

Glancing upward, Henry continued speaking. "We will stay strong in our faith. If we keep fear from us and stay in the light of God, we can beat whatever is in this house."

"Then my prayers will be with you," Father Thalheimer said. "I will ask that God grant you peace from whatever spirits dwell in this house."

Two nights later, however, the evil within the house focused itself into an irresistible force.

Henry Salvato had been upstairs shaving while Carol worked at some household chore on the first floor. Although he had been feeling distinct unease, Henry did not become conscious of the foreboding whispers floating through the air until they reached a greater volume than he had previously heard. They seemed to encircle him and close in on him, until the suggestion of evil became so strong that he feared for his wife.

Dropping his razor, Henry rushed to the stairs, where a frightening scene confronted him. Carol stood on the landing, transfixed with terror. Her limbs had stiffened and her hands clutched frantically at her side. The veins along her neck had swollen and were darkly prominent. Her head was thrown back. Her eyes bulged with terror, and her mouth gaped in a scream that could not be heard.

Henry knew he must help her. But when he moved down the stairs he ran directly into an invisible force that would not allow him to pass. It seemed to shroud him like an unseen net, holding him fast, while his hands desperately flailed the air and his feet worked futilely.

At last one of his hands found the banister, and with it as a lever, Henry summoned all his strength to hurl his body into the palpable wall of evil.

Lunging, he broke through, and instantly the sounds of his wife's screams filled the house.

The next moment, he stood by her side, holding her close as she sobbed into his shoulder. She, too, had been gripped by the whispering evil and seized by its terror.

Sandi!

In the same speechless instant both parents were alerted to the danger that faced their daughter. Henry and Carol ran back up the stairs and into their daughter's room.

Sandi was cowering in a corner, tears streaming from eyes wide with terror. Standing just before her, his back arched, his green eyes glowing, his growl indicating his resolve, Blue Angel provided determined interference for whatever evil stalked his young mistress.

The Salvatos had had enough. Without bothering to pack, they grabbed Sandi and Steven and left the house—with Blue Angel running just behind them, as if covering their retreat.

A week later, when the Salvatos returned with some friends in the bright light of afternoon to collect their belongings, the friends, too, heard the strange whispers and thumps. Once they had finished packing, the Salvatos said they would forfeit all the money they had put into the house of evil before they ever entered it again.

*   *   *

In my more than thirty years as a chronicler and researcher of the strange, the unusual, and the unknown, I have found that certain houses can act as reservoirs of emotions from past occupants, and that certain rooms can become psychically charged. Nearly everyone has had the experience of walking into a "happy" house, a "depressing" room, or a room that appears quite ordinary in every respect until it seems suddenly to erupt with distinct impressions of unease or distaste.

Sensitive animals such as dogs—and especially cats—can perceive these negative impressions and may be unable to interpret them as anything other than a threat to themselves and their owners.

Sensitive humans, those possessed of the proper telepathic affinity with the implanted memory-patterns of a particular environment, may enter a certain room and receive an influence from those who lived there before. They may experience the emotions, share the impulses; if the impressions are strong enough, they may even catch "glimpses" of the former inhabitants—that is, ghosts.

As yet our science is inadequate to define precisely what factors must be present before a dramatic haunting—such as the one the Salvato family experienced—can occur. For the present, we must theorize that an environment is somehow psychically impregnated by a living, physical entity in a state of emotional intensity. Therefore, a certain house or room can be so "charged" that even years later those same impulses can be received by a sensitive human being—or a sensitive animal.

Some researchers hypothesize that extreme emotional states, such as great sorrow, overwhelming fear, and intense hatred, increase the "radiation" of these influences and make their primary and secondary results more powerful. An extreme emotional experience, such as that of a murder which took place in a paroxysm of hatred and terror, would be expected to create the deepest psychic impression and have the strongest power to evoke similar emotions in a percipient. It may then be put forward that some houses, because of the highly charged emotions of certain deeds of violence or enmity perpetrated within their walls, have become respositories of hatred and reservoirs of evil.

Fear, sorrow, and hatred unfortunately seem to be stronger emotions than happiness and contentment. While a sensitive person may feel warm and secure in a "happy" room, one seldom gains any clear impression of what made that particular room so joyful.

Or is it the dark side of our personality that is most easily reached by psychic impressions? Fear, Edgar Allan Poe believed, was the most primitive of emotions and the easiest to evoke in a fellow human being. It is sobering to contemplate that what we may leave behind us after we are gone is our worst impression.

Spirits of Cats That Came Back to Give Comfort

My late colleague Professor Ian Currie was not only a respected professor at the University of Toronto but he was also a world-renowned psychical researcher who had investigated sightings of spirit entities for many years.

"Ghosts of cats are very much like ghosts of humans," Currie said. "I believe that they return from the afterlife primarily to give comfort to grieving loved ones they've left behind."

Consider the case of the woman in Toronto who, in 1968, lost the Persian cat she had adored for seventeen years. Her entire family went into mourning for the beloved pet; they all knew how much their mother had loved him.

On the third evening after the cat's passing, the woman was awakened in her bed by the familiar sound of her Persian's purr. With tears of joy streaming down her cheeks, she next felt the delicate touch of her cat's tiny feet moving over her shoulder as he prepared to snuggle around her, just as he had done in life.

The next morning, she came to the breakfast table filled with excitement over her experience and eager to share the good news of her cat's spirit return. But before she could utter a word, her daughter was telling everyone of her own marvelous encounter with the world beyond death. The cat had visited her during the night as well.

Within a few more days, the spirit of the Persian cat had manifested as a ghostly apparition seen by many witnesses.

"I have seen him come through the wall from my daughter's room," the cat's owner said. "His eyes shine like jewels, and there is a bluish light and little starlike sparks all around him. He bumps me in the face and gives me his soft little kisses."

Professor Ian Currie cited the impressive case of an English aristocrat, Sir Ernest Bennett, who had become extremely attached to his purebred Persian, Smokey.

Saddened by Smokey's death, Sir Ernest and his sister were startled to observe the very distinctive shape of the Persian cat limping across the lawn outside their mansion. Smokey appeared to be ill, but she was unmistakably their beloved cat.

Sir Ernest ran outside to reclaim his dear Smokey—but the cat vanished.

Could they both have been seeing things? Sir Ernest wondered over and over whether he and his sister had somehow projected their sorrow into a collective hallucination.

But then a family friend insisted that he had seen Sir Ernest's Smoky walking the grounds of the estate.

Desperately, Sir Ernest instructed his gardener to open Smokey's grave to be certain that she had truly died.

Later, the apparitions ceased, and the Bennett family conjectured that when they had seen Smokey's ghost, it had been because her spirit was still confused and unaware of her own death.

Psychic News, an international newspaper on spiritual matters published in London, has reported for years that the ghosts of dead cats often return from another dimension of reality to visit the human families they have left behind on the earthly plane. According to many published accounts, ghostly cats have jumped on their owners' beds at night, materialized on their laps, and left nose smudges on windows.

One cat owner wrote to Psychic News to testify that his deceased cat's frequent visits from beyond the grave filled him with peace and love.

Another woman testified that a ten-minute materialization of her cat from the Other Side had enabled her to shake a lingering illness. Within two days, she was feeling better. Not only had her physical condition improved, but her fortunes had also taken a more positive turn.

The Cat That Spoke in Tongues

Although I raised the possibility of demonic possession of cats in Chapter 5, and chose to skirt the cosmological implications of nonphysical entities assuming control of a physical body, I know of a most interesting case in 1978 in a small town in New Mexico in which a family came to believe that their large Siamese cat was possessed by the poltergeistic activity in their home.

The word *poltergeist* in German means a ghost that throws things; in the parlance of contemporary psychical research the term has come to represent a paranormal disturbance characterized by explosive psychokinetic manifestations—*i.e.*, objects being tossed around, mysterious fires breaking out, large pieces of furniture being moved, and so on.

The manifestations that beset the Brian Clancy home began on what had been a quiet evening in mid-January. The initial demonstration of the unseen energy force had startled members of the Clancy family, as they watched a ceramic flowerpot lift itself from a shelf and crash through a nearby window.

During the evening meal, a sugar bowl floated up to the chandelier and dumped its contents into the electric candle holders. Pictures tumbled off their hooks and crashed to the floor. An old brass incense burner flew six feet off a bookshelf. Some recently acquired Native American pottery that had been left on a bed was smashed to pieces by an unseen force.

A case of soda bottles exploded like a string of firecrackers. A small table in the dining room suddenly became animated and danced on two legs across the room.

And then the pebbles began flying.

Small multicolored stones appeared out of thin air and began to pelt Brian Clancy, his wife, Mary, and their two children, Angela, twelve, and Sean, five. Angela and her Siamese cat, Bonnie Jean, seemed to be struck the most often, but few of the pebbles landed with enough force to raise even a temporary welt or bruise. It was as if the stones floated toward them.

By the time the police arrived, a barrage of rocks was falling on the roof of the Clancy home. The officers listened to the family's testimony with expressions of disbelief. Although they could hear stones dropping on the roof—but could see nothing because it was dark—they concluded that some birds must be dropping pebbles as they flew over. They promised to have an animal control officer come by in the morning to check things out in the daylight.

After a night of iced-tea glasses shattering, ashtrays smashing themselves against walls, and a stack of firewood exploding and sending bits of bark and pulp across the room like shrapnel, Brian Clancy placed a much more urgent call to the authorities.

The police department's crime laboratory could find no trace of any explosives having been inserted in the moving or exploding objects. City highway personnel tested for earth tremors with a seismograph and found nothing. A friend of Clancy's, a radio and television repairman, blamed the trouble on high-frequency radio waves, but his sensitive equipment could record none.

And then, that night, Bonnie Jean, the four-year-old Siamese, suddenly began to scream like a banshee. As the family stood by watching incredulously, the cat began writhing across the floor as if she were a snake—and hissing loudly.

But the most horrible—and seemingly impossible—manifestation occurred when a bizarre babble began issuing from the Siamese—a mumbling gibberish that sounded for all the world as if she were speaking a jumble of human tongues.

"We could not prove that Bonnie Jean was saying words," Mary Clancy said. "But it actually did seem as though the cat were speaking in tongues. I have never heard such sounds coming from the mouth of a cat!"

Angela continued to hold her pet in her lap, attempting to soothe her during her most dramatic gyrations. "Bonnie Jean's eyes rolled around in her head, and she made these terrible noises," Angela said. "She acted a lot like the little girl in the movie *The Exorcist.*"

Brian Clancy contacted their pastor, who offered prayers but quickly bowed out when he heard the cat hissing and saw her writhing like a snake.

"He said the matter was beyond his theological expertise," Mary said. "And he didn't even hear Bonnie Jean speaking in tongues."

Bonnie Jean's guttural roars and screams were becoming louder and more persistent, and with them came a fusillade of airborne objects, such as knives, forks, and stones, directed at Angela. Although the twelve-year-old was never seriously injured by the missiles, she was thoroughly frightened.

This may all read like a combination of trickery and hallucination, intensified by the power of suggestion. However, witnesses to such poltergeistic activity are very often highly educated and responsible persons who have perceived for themselves unexplained sights and sounds—objects that move without any traceable causes, and in some cases rappings and voices that exhibit intelligence.

The late psychoanalyst, Nandor Fodor believed there was no doubt that the poltergeist was a part of our reality. Based on his investigations, Fodor pointed out that the lifetime of a poltergeist was usually limited to a few weeks or months.

The poltergeist becomes, as it were, an uninvited guest, moving in to play its pranks and work its horrors on an unappreciative family.

The difference between a *geist* (ghost) and a poltergeist, in Fodor's evaluation, is that a ghost haunts a house and a poltergeist haunts a person. "The poltergeist is not a ghost," he said, "but a bundle of projected repressions."

Not all researchers agree with Fodor that a poltergeist always has to do with the repressions of the living and never with the anger or frustrations of the dead; but the majority of psychical investigators probably do concur that the center of the poltergeistic activity is usually associated with a teenage member of the family, more often a girl than a boy. An exhaustive study of poltergeist manifestations convinced noted researcher Harry Price that the sexual changes inherent in puberty are frequently associated with either the beginning or the cessation of the phenomena.

The English writer Sacheverell Sitwell wrote his opinion that the poltergeist finds its center of energy in the person of an adolescent, who performs the effects, both consciously and unconsciously, "being gifted for the time being with something approaching criminal cunning. The particular direction of this power is always toward the secret or concealed weaknesses of the spirit . . . the obscene or erotic recesses of the soul.

"The mysteries of puberty, that trance or dozing of the psyche before it awakes to adult life, is a favorite playground for the poltergeist."

Whether or not the poltergeist that visited the Clancy family in New Mexico shifted its "playground" from Angela to Bonnie Jean, the Siamese, must remain the subject of academic and esoteric conjecture.

A Navajo medicine priest and healer summoned by the Clancy family declared that the evil spirit of a snake-worshipping cultist from long ago had possessed the cat. The medicine priest performed a lengthy ritual of chanting and prayer, which he explained beforehand was designed to bring the entity peace and to free it to travel on to the land of the grandfathers.

"Whatever the man did, it seemed to have a calming effect on Bonnie Jean and the disturbances in our home," Brian Clancy said. "The cat's growls, grunts, and roars grew quieter. And that bizarre babbling sound it emitted ceased altogether."

Bonnie Jean appeared to fall into a deep sleep as she was cradled in Angela's arms, and when she awakened in ten minutes or so, she looked up at her young mistress and began to purr.

"Hey, everybody," Angela smiled. "Bonnie Jean is back. She's her old self again."

Whether it was the power of the Navajo medicine priest's ritual of exorcism, or whether the energy of the poltergeist had simply expended itself, the Clancy family's ordeal had ended.

Curse of the Cat Mummy in England's Old Mill Hotel

Residents of Sudbury, England, believe that some ancient curse was set on them when a mummified cat was removed from beneath the floorboards of the historic Mill Hotel during renovations and not quickly and properly replaced.

When builder Arthur Kemp found the mummified feline, he was puzzled. He could tell that the thing was very old, and he wondered whether some taxidermist of ages past had hidden away a particularly significant stuffed cat for some long-forgotten purpose.

Local historians to whom Kemp brought the mummified cat and a batch of questions told him it had been a common practice in centuries past to imprison a live cat in a new building to protect it from evil spirits.

"It was a sort of sacrifice," one old-timer informed Kemp. "About three hundred years ago, it was a regular thing to lock up a cat so that its spirit could keep the evil ones away.

"I've found about a dozen or so in other old houses and hotels in this area," he told the builder, "and I always put them back where I found them. I would advise you, sir, to do the same thing!"

The owners of the Mill Hotel found this bit of local folklore most interesting, but they decided to put the mummified cat on display in an art shop they owned.

"Don't you think we ought to pay some attention to the old-timer's advice?" Kemp asked them. "Why don't I just put the old puss back where I found it?"

The hotel owners had hired Kemp because he had been highly recommended as a fine builder. They politely informed him that they did not require his services as a decorator.

A few weeks later, the art store burned down. The cat mummy stood silent and erect among the smoking ruins—not a hair on its ancient coat so much as singed.

Kemp learned later that the mummy was given to a friend of the owners who lived in a farmhouse outside Sudbury. Within a few weeks, that house was also severely damaged by a mysterious fire that broke out around the mummified feline remains.

Incredibly, the hotel owners then gave the mummy back to Arthur Kemp—who, even more incredibly, accepted it. The builder was not keen on placing the object in his home or in his office, however. He decided he would keep it in the trunk of his car to see whether he couldn't temper the power of the curse.

He forgot about the old mummy in the press of his work— and then had three automobile accidents in a week.

Around the same time, he heard that the section of the Mill Hotel where he had discovered the centuries-old remains had collapsed. Once again, Kemp was called in to handle the repair work.

Just before he got at the task, the old hotel was taken over by new owners who were much more receptive to the builder's account of the curse of the cat mummy. They didn't want any part of the bad luck that had been circulating ever since the remains had been disturbed. They even asked Kemp to construct a special niche for the mummy and to place it back under the hotel floorboards where he had found it.

Once the builder had respectfully replaced the mummy beneath the repaired floorboards, things in Sudbury seemed to return to normal.

But then, the present manager of the hotel said, as unwise as it seemed, he decided to give the mummy a good cleaning.

That night the sprinkler system in the kitchen mysteriously came on, drenched the place, and caused thousands of dollars' worth of damage.

"I'll never touch the creature's mummy again," the manager vowed. "It is apparent that every time the mummy is disturbed, misfortune is certain to follow."

7

Cats with Weird Talents

On a November night in 1989, the police in Tulsa were puzzled by an emergency call that seemed to be nothing more than moans and high-pitched yowling.

The computer display system showed them the exact address from which the call was coming. When Officer Dale Ferber arrived on the scene, he found a darkened house; no one responded to his ringing of the front doorbell or his vigorous knocking.

Fearing the worst, Ferber called for a backup officer, and the two received authorization to break in through the front door.

Once inside the house, the officers heard the reported moaning and yowling—and were able to identify the sounds as those of a troubled cat. When they entered the kitchen they found a very anxious Siamese tangled up in a twelve-foot telephone cord, lying on the floor next to a toppled counter telephone.

"In its struggles to get free," Ferber said, "the cord had tightened about the cat's throat. If it hadn't dialed 911, it would have strangled itself in very short order."

And how had Simba the Siamese managed to dial the emergency number?

"The way we figure it," Ferber explained, "the Siamese must have jumped up on the counter, got tangled in the telephone cord, fell to the floor, and pulled the phone with him. When cat and phone hit the floor, the receiver got knocked off; and as the cat struggled more and more to free himself, he stepped on the button that had been preprogrammed to dial 911."

Simba's owners, Allan and Jayne Horn, had been out to dinner and a movie. They returned home to find their front door badly damaged and a note of explanation from the police.

The Horns expressed their gratitude to the officers for having saved their cat's life. "A new door we can always get," Jayne Horn said, "but our Simba is one in a million."

On October 20, 1990, police in Troy, New York, broke into an apartment after their 911 emergency number received what sounded like a call from someone badly injured and too weak to speak. When they got inside, they found to their astonishment that the caller must have been saying, *"Meow"* not "Me . . . *ow!"*

Bill Krauss's cat, Yeager, had apparently pawed the pad of a preprogrammed push-button telephone that automatically dialed the police emergency number. Although the dispatcher heard no intelligible voice, he traced the call to Krauss's apartment.

When the officers who were dispatched to the scene couldn't find a building superintendent or break down the door, they cut through a window screen. Once inside, they found no accident or crime victim, just a contented cat that obviously had been playing with the telephone.

Bill Krauss thought it was someone's idea of a weird joke when he returned to his apartment to find a note tacked to his door. According to Krauss, the note said, "Your cat called the police. We had to force entry to check the apartment."

Police Sergeant Robert Paul said no charges were being contemplated against Yeager, the cat, for filing a false report.

Marvalee Wagner of Alameda, California, said her cat Rusty is an accomplished thief of underwear and socks.

"Rusty really has a thing for laundry," Wagner said. "She steals sweaters, hats, undies—but she's especially fond of socks!"

Once, Wagner said, Rusty went on an all-out weekend raid and brought home forty-two socks, mostly women's knee-highs.

Wagner said she has long since given up attempting to track down the victims of her little desperado. She just piles the assorted laundry at her front door, and the neighbors come over and reclaim their stolen articles.

Missy, a Siamese with a flair for tap-dancing on computer keys, was performing an intricate fandango on her owner's home computer in Los Angeles when she accidentally punched in a secret five-letter code that accessed a business memory bank—and instantly erased $50,000 worth of account files.

A company spokesman, decidedly not a fan of Siamese dancing, said the business would have to revamp its entire computer system.

Gypsy has attained local fame in Washington, D.C., as a feline alarm clock. The black and white tomcat awakens his mistress at precisely 6:45 A.M. each morning—and can even make the adjustment to Daylight Saving Time.

Sally Longbaugh of Dearborn, Michigan, numbers among the

many cat lovers who claim to own felines that speak actual, discernible words in brief phrases.

"Beau clearly says, 'Let me out,' 'I love you,' 'Eat now, Mommy,' and several other phrases," Longbaugh said.

Raymond Long of Kansas City insists he has built up a strong telepathic link with his cat, Fred, which enables them to communicate even over great distances.

"Once when I was in Baltimore on business," Long said, "I received the distinct impression that there had been a small fire in our apartment. I felt Fred's fear and his consternation. I could feel that he wanted me with him. I also saw that he had my most expensive wristwatch—one I never take with me on the road—in his bed with him."

That night when Raymond telephoned the friend whom he had asked to check in on Fred, she told him that there had indeed been a small fire in his apartment building.

"I think it was two or three floors below your place," she said. "I could tell that old Fred was pretty shook up about it, though. You know, the smoke and the sirens and everything. And a funny thing, Fred had your favorite wristwatch in his mouth when I came to feed him. It was like he was going to save your most valuable belonging in case of fire."

Henry Craig, Glendale, California, is one of many cat lovers who vow that their felines have the remarkable ability of astral traveling, leaving their physical bodies to be seen in two places at the same time.

"On several occasions, my fiancée has sworn that she has seen Burt in her place when he is curled up at my feet sleeping," Craig said. "My mother, too, has insisted that she has seen Burt watching her from the shadows when she goes to bed some nights. I know that he astral projects in his sleep and that his soul-body looks in on those people we both love the most."

The Astral Awareness of Cats

In their book *Psychic Phenomena*, Dorothy Bomar Bradley, M.D., and Robert A. Bradley, M.D., tell of a bachelor friend, a great cat fancier, who had a black cat as his companion for many years. It had been the cat's habit to run to the refrigerator whenever he was hungry and pace back and forth in front of the door, meowing. When their friend moved to a new apartment, however, the cat would not come near the refrigerator—even if the most tempting food was being proffered there.

The Bradleys' friend informed them that his cat seemed to be afraid of that area and would sit and stare at the refrigerator for long periods. When the bachelor described his cat's peculiar behavior to his landlady, the woman told him that the former tenant had been a widow who had disposed of the refrigerator and stove and elected to eat all of her meals out of the apartment. In the recessed area where the refrigerator had stood, she had placed a small table with candles. She had conducted séances at the spot during which she communicated regularly with the spirit of her deceased husband.

The Bradleys theorize that their friend's cat may have possessed an "astral awareness," that is, an "instinctual function . . . of the subconscious animal brain" that enables it to pierce the barrier "between the unobstructed and obstructed universe, between the astral world and the earth world." The cat in the apartment, lacking human reason and a logical, conscious mind, did not know how to accept the entities he perceived and became frightened by these noncorporeal beings that made no sounds and carried no identifying smells.

Lyall Watson, author of the best-seller *Supernature*, relates the following account of an experiment involving the varying abilities of animals to perceive the unknown in his book *The Romeo Error: A Matter of Life and Death*.

Summoned to investigate an allegedly haunted house in Kentucky, Robert Morris of Duke University brought with him a collection of living "ghost detectors" in the form of a dog, a cat, a rat, and a rattlesnake. One by one, each of the animals was taken by its owner into a room in which a murder had been committed.

The dog walked only two feet into the room, then uncharacteristically began to snarl at his owner and backed out the door. No amount of cajoling or promised reward could induce the dog to reenter the room.

The cat's owner carried her pet into the room, and when the cat reached the same spot where the dog had turned tail, he leaped up on his owner's shoulders. A few moments later, he jumped to the floor, directed his attention toward a corner of the room, and spent several minutes hissing, spitting, and staring at an unoccupied chair.

The rat showed no signs of sensing anything, but the rattlesnake instantly coiled into an attack stance while focusing on the same empty chair.

"None of the three responsive animals produced a comparable reaction in any other room of the house," Watson writes. "The relative acuteness of the cat's sense system may account for the fact that witches use them as familiars, as aerials or extensions of their own senses for picking up subtle signals."

*A Mysterious Cat
Appears to Free Her
from the Grip of a
Terrible Nightmare*

Catherine Layton experienced an eerie foreboding the moment she set foot in the lovely cabin on the Virginia coast.
The July day in 1987 was bright and sunny, but the kitchen
area—and especially the bedroom—seemed dark and sinister,
even though dazzling sunshine streamed through the open
windows.

"Is this the only cabin that's available?" Layton asked Mrs.
Pickron, the landlady, who seemed to be avoiding eye contact
with her.

"You know this is our busiest season," the tall, thin woman
answered. "Just about everybody wants to be on the beach in
July. I told you when you wrote that you were lucky we had
any vacancies. We've got a waiting list, you know, so if you
don't want it . . ."

Layton had looked forward to a pleasant two weeks in this
quaint resort town, where she might receive inspiration to
write a number of free-lance magazine articles. Fifty weeks out
of the year, as society editor for a small-town newspaper in
Illinois, she wrote about weddings, engagements, graduations,
Rotary dinners, and funerals. For two weeks she wanted to
write for herself.

"No, no, the cabin is fine," Layton assured Mrs. Pickron. "It's just that it feels . . . strange to me."

The landlady raised an eyebrow and pursed her lips before she answered. "My husband, Lester, and I work hard to make these cabins pleasant and cheerful. I gave you Cabin Sixteen because it is one of our loveliest. Maybe it's the ocean that troubles you . . . the sounds of the waves and all. Takes some Midwestern folk—who normally hear only cricket and critter sounds—a while to get used to the noise of the surf."

Layton had lived in Illinois for only four years; she had grown up in La Jolla, California, with the sounds, smells, and rhythm of the surf. "I'm certain I will adjust in the days and nights to come," she said. "The cabin is just fine."

"In order to keep the budget tight, I had already decided to cook most of my meals at the cabin," Layton said in her account of her remarkable experience. "But on my first night by the ocean, I made up my mind to treat myself to an elaborate meal at an elegant seafood restaurant I had passed a few miles back. I returned to the cabin about three hours later, full of excellent lobster and exquisite wine."

Although the evening was quite warm, on her return to the cabin Layton noticed that it felt cold and damp.

"But I had driven over three hundred miles that day, and my fatigue, coupled with the good food and the wine, made me think about nothing else but collapsing into bed and getting a good night's sleep," she said. "Tomorrow morning would bring a beach walk, some sun, and a good session at the typewriter."

But the night did not bless Layton with a restful sleep.

"In a terrifying dream, I was lying in bed when I heard a strange shuffling sound. I looked up to see a dark human shape coming toward me from the kitchen. It was one of those really nasty dreams—you know, the kind where you can't move and you can't run and you can't even scream. This thing kept coming closer and closer, and then I could hear that it was calling my name over and over.

"It smelled of seaweed and brine, and as it bent over me, I could see this horrible skull-like face leering at me."

Layton awakened drenched with sweat, strands of her hair matted to her damp forehead. "I blamed the bad dream on too many glasses of wine," she admitted, "but I got up, went to the bathroom, then turned on every light in the cabin so I could go back to sleep."

The dream haunted her all the next day. She took her beach walk, lay in the sun for twenty minutes or so, then tried to work on one of her articles.

"I decided not to be too hard on myself. After all, the days before my vacation had been exhausting. The editor had insisted that I cover every Fourth of July function in town and have all the copy on his desk before I left on the sixth. And then there had been the straight-through drive from Illinois to Virginia, stopping only for catnaps at the safest-looking rest areas. I really owed it to myself to spend at least one day doing nothing before I got to work on the article."

That night, in spite of a pleasant evening spent in delightful conversation with the young honeymooning couple in the cabin to the left of hers, the awful nightmare returned to terrify her.

"This time I seemed to have a telepathic link with the rotted corpse from the sea," Layton said. "It . . . he . . . had once lived in the cabin. He had stayed there frequently with his wife.

"Then there had been a terrible fight, a nasty, shouting argument, over her acts of infidelity. At last, she admitted her unfaithfulness and scornfully laughed at him, mocking his ineffectualness as a lover. Humiliated, he had run out on to the beach and into the pounding surf. An undercurrent caught him just a few yards out, and he had drowned.

"It was becoming clear what he wanted with me," Layton

continued. "Fiery red eyes glowed lustfully in the empty skull sockets. Since all women were nothing but sluts in his warped view, he now sought to prove himself an effective and virile lover with every woman who occupied that cabin. The same cabin that had served as his stage for heartbreak and humiliation would now forever be the platform for the proving of his manhood."

Layton tried desperately to awaken from the grip of the terrible nightmare. "I could not seem to wake up! And he had begun to press his cold, wet, clawlike fingers into my shoulders. Seawater and saliva dripped from his partially decomposed lips as he brought his ghastly face closer and closer to mine. I could feel him beginning to move his sea-drenched body on top of my own. And all about me was the salty stench of the sea.

"At last, with a supreme effort of will, I managed to awaken, to free myself from the cold grip of the ugly, obscene, animated corpse."

This time, at four o'clock in the morning, Layton could not blame the hideous nightmare on too much lobster and too many glasses of wine.

"What concerned me most was the horrible thought that if I should have the dream again, would I be able to wake up?" she said. "I suddenly felt as though I was in a movie like *A Nightmare on Elm Street* and a monster as bad as Freddy Krueger was trying to get me while I dreamed. Would I have to try to stay awake and not dream, like the teenagers in that movie?

"And if I should fall asleep and dream and be unable to awake in time, would I somehow be imprisoned within the nightmare until the wretched, horrible thing had its way with me? And even worse, might I somehow be trapped inside the dream forever and never awaken?"

Layton brewed herself some strong coffee, drank several

cups, then went outside to spend the few remaining hours until dawn on the beach.

By first light, she was chiding herself for allowing an overactive imagination to transform her into a frightened wimp. Being trapped inside a dream while a lustful corpse tried to have its way with her—what nonsense!

If she told Mrs. Pickron about the nightmares, the landlady would call it a Midwesterner's trouble adjusting to the sound of the pounding surf. If she confessed the dream to the honeymooners, barely out of their teens, they would snicker and whisper behind her back that she, an old maid of thirty-five, was sexually frustrated.

Still, as much as she tried to rationalize, there was something so strange, so real, so terrifying about those nightmares.

It was precisely at this moment, as she struggled between reason and abject fear, that Layton felt something soft and furry rubbing against her bare ankle. Startled out of her thoughts, she could not suppress a small squeal of relief when she beheld the exceptionally large Maine coon cat that had joined her.

"In the two days that I had been there, I had seen a number of dogs running on the beach, but not one cat," she said. "I had no idea where this one had come from, but his company was most welcome."

The sort of person who is compelled to give a name to every creature large and small that made her acquaintance, Layton simply called the large cat Buddy.

"Buddy followed me back into the cabin and did not hesitate to accept the food I offered him. Within a few minutes it was obvious that he was making himself at home. Somehow I felt better already, just knowing that I would not face the night alone. My Buddy was there with me."

The cat stayed by Layton's side throughout the day, joining her on a beach walk, gingerly approaching the foaming surf as it broke on the sand.

"When we met Mrs. Pickron and her husband, Lester, on the beach, neither of them could ever remember seeing Buddy before—or any cat that looked like him—in the area," Layton said. "Lester offered that he himself 'fancied' dogs."

That night when she got into bed, Buddy jumped up on a nearby chair and assumed a position of vigilance.

"It was the strangest thing," Layton said. "Buddy showed no signs of intending to sleep. It was as if he were on guard duty."

Weary from lack of rest the night before and calmed by the presence of her guardian, Layton permitted herself to drift into a state of deep relaxation. Within moments she had fallen fast asleep.

"I must have slept for hours. I had a number of brief dreams about my work back on the newspaper, and I was in the midst of a pleasant memory re-creation of a summer vacation trip to Yellowstone Park that I had taken with my parents when I was around thirteen, when I suddenly became aware of a dark, shadowy form following me," she said. "A cold hand reached out to grab my arm, and I was pulled back to the Virginia seashore. I was thrown on my back to the coarse sand, and then *he* was on top of me, pinning my arms above my thrashing head, pressing my struggling body to his evil will.

"Waves of nausea surged over me as his rotting lips tried to find my own. I knew I must wake up. I must free myself from his nightmarish hold on me. I must summon all of my willpower to escape from him."

Layton remembered how the entity laughed at her puny efforts to resist his amorous advances. " 'It's no use,' he laughed at me. 'I have you now!' "

That was when she became aware of Buddy yowling into her ear, and she felt herself momentarily jerked from the terrible grip of the nightmare demon. The obscene entity roared a string of blistering profanities, then pulled her back into the awful dream.

"I was suddenly the object of an incredible tug-of-war," she said. "I wanted to wake up and be free of the nemesis from the nightmare, but the terrible creature's hold on me had become too great to enable Buddy's screeches to fully awaken me. My guardian must have sensed this, because that was when he bit me hard and deep on my shoulder. The pain seared through my nerves and slammed hard into my brain, shattering the ghastly dream into a million pieces of harmless unreality."

Layton sat up in bed and opened her eyes to the most beautiful sunrise she had ever seen in her life. She had escaped from the terror of the night. Her guardian cat had somehow sensed her peril and had acted to free her from the demon's grip with the most immediate means at its disposal.

"It didn't quite seem to be over," Layton said. "The large cat appeared to be chasing something into a shadowy corner of the bedroom. He sat up on his haunches, pawed the air with his claws extended, and emitted one of the loudest, most startling cries that I have ever heard from a cat's mouth.

"Buddy must have sent the evil thing packing with that fierce battle cry, because he got back down on all fours and, seeming quite satisfied with himself, walked to the kitchen to lap at the bowl of milk I had set out for him in the evening."

A short while later, as Layton was fixing some breakfast for herself, Buddy jumped up on the kitchen counter and brought his head close to her own. "He seemed to be focusing his large green eyes on mine, and almost as though I were hearing words directly in my brain, he was telling me that everything was all right now. I was safe. The nightmare would not return."

Catherine cradled Buddy in her arms and began to weep. "His pink little tongue touched my cheek twice; then he jumped free of my arms and headed toward the cabin door. I called after him, but he kept walking, mindful of his own schedule of activities, his own mission in life."

She never saw Buddy again. "I spent some part of every remaining day looking for him," she said. "I asked about him, but no one ever recalled seeing a large Maine coon cat anywhere on the beach.

"I'm convinced that Buddy appeared solely for the purpose of freeing me from the nightmare's demonic control over me. Maybe he was my guardian angel."

For the remainder of her vacation, Layton slept soundly, her dreams untroubled. She also managed to complete three articles.

When she was checking out at the main desk, Lester Pickron provided her with the capper to the whole affair.

"Well," he said, smiling, "I guess you beat the jinx of Cabin Sixteen."

Layton frowned as she asked what he meant. She noticed that Mrs. Pickron was nowhere to be seen.

"Yeah, the missus and I called it a jinx, anyway," Lester said. "About five or six years ago, we had a nice young woman die in her sleep in that cabin. The doctors could never find any reason for her death. She just up and died. Ever since then, though, every single gal who rents that cabin has complained of awful nightmares and refused to stay more than a night. It's been a really weird thing, because we never told any of the other ladies about the woman's strange death. We've tried to keep it quiet, that's for sure."

Layton entertained brief thoughts of throwing both Pickrons into the ocean.

"Anyway, Ms. Layton"—Lester smiled again—"thanks for breaking the jinx."

Layton wanted to tell him to thank a mysterious Maine coon cat that had somehow heard her silent prayers for help and had come to her rescue—but she knew that neither of her insensitive hosts would understand.

The Healing Powers of Cats

Hundreds of cases document the astonishing healing powers cats possess. Cats have been reported to rouse children from deep comas, to help the mentally ill regain stability, and to bring new hope to those who had accepted only pain and despair as their lifelong companions.

Judy Kaplanis of Topeka, Kansas, had always believed that her fourteen-year-old tomcat, Rodney, had a special gift for making her feel better. Kaplanis, now thirty, had had Rodney since she was sixteen, and he had always had the knack of cheering her up whenever she was gloomy or depressed.

"There was just something about that big old yellow cat that always made me feel good," she said. "And then, a few years ago, I began to notice that not only would Rodney chase my blues away, he would take away my headaches and upset stomachs.

"My kids noticed it, too, because they started calling for

Rodney to sleep with them whenever they were coming down with a cold or had a stomachache. Even my husband, Jim, picks Rodney up and sets him on his lap when he comes home extra tired from work. After about an hour of stroking Rodney's yellow fur, Jim always says he feels better and more invigorated."

Judy Kaplanis said that visitors to their home who might not feel well when they arrive usually leave feeling much better.

"A friend of mine suffered from terrible insomnia," she said. "Night after night she would toss and turn something awful. Well, one day she came to visit, and Rodney jumped on her lap. She didn't seem to mind, so I just let him sit there so I could see what would happen. When I saw her three days later, she said she had been sleeping at nights like a baby."

A local school administrator suffered so badly from arthritis that she feared she would be forced to resign her position before the end of the semester. After one visit to the Kaplanis home and after holding Rodney on her lap for a while, the administrator's condition was so much improved that she is able to lead a normal life.

On occasion, Rodney's presence has healed other cats, dogs, even parakeets.

"Some people may think that I'm crazy talking like this about Rodney," Judy Kaplanis said. "But I truly believe that my cat has the gift of healing."

Gretchen Tynar of Scottsdale, Arizona, relies on her Persian cat, Prince, to relieve her minor aches and pains.

"If I have a bad sore throat, Prince knows intuitively to drape himself across my neck when I lie down," she said. "My throat will feel better in minutes. The same is true if I have a stomach upset, a backache, or a headache. The moment I lie down, Prince goes immediately to the part of my anatomy that is troubling me."

Gretchen believes Prince absorbs the pain, then releases it in another dimension of reality. "I know this will sound really weird, but I have watched him walk into a particular corner in the sitting room of my apartment—and just disappear. I mean, like that, he is gone.

"Then maybe in an hour or less, he'll be out in the hallway scratching at the door to be let in. There is no way that he can get out of the apartment except through the door, and I keep it locked at all times.

"So how do you explain it?" she asked. "How can he walk into a corner of the sitting room, disappear, and a few minutes later be out in the hall? My healing cat is also a multidimensional cat!"

Owning a Cat Can Lower Your Blood Pressure

Owning a cat can slash your risk of heart disease, lower your blood pressure, and reduce your cholesterol levels. According to numerous studies pet owners have significantly reduced levels of known risk factors for cardiovascular disease.

A 1991 University of Pennsylvania study of heart attack victims showed that owning a pet can mean the difference between death and recovery. Doctors found that simply stroking a cat can reduce blood pressure and heart rate. The rhythmic process of petting a cat can have the same effect on a stressed-out patient as certain relaxation techniques, including meditation.

Dr. Leo Bustad of the College of Veterinary Medicine at Washington State University has expressed dismay that it has taken such a long time for some people to become convinced of the value of domestic animals like cats in improving health. Pets have amazing healing powers, Bustad has commented, and their very presence seems to be able to block pain.

Researchers have theorized that the bond that develops between a cat owner and his or her pet centers on touching—and in many instances that may be the real key to a cat's healing powers. Very often the mentally ill have isolated themselves from the touch of other human beings. Sometimes a patient with a debilitating disease has been deprived of loving touch for far too long. The cat with its friendly purr is much less threatening than another human being, who may respond to an affectionate gesture with a rebuff.

A recent survey conducted by Dr. Erika Friedmann of Brooklyn College revealed that the survival rate for heart patients with pets is much higher than for those without animal companionship. Friedmann says she is disappointed that such awareness comes slowly for many patients, who want a magic drug in a capsule, rather than a loyal, playful pet.

Jane Bailey's Remarkable Feline Healers, Rogan and Gus

British spiritualist Jane Bailey has been privileged to serve as the human catalyst for two remarkable feline healers, Rogan and Gus.

In the early 1970s, Bailey began to notice that sick people appeared to feel much better after her cat, Rogan, had spent some time with them. It seemed to her that Rogan had been blessed by some higher power with the gift of healing.

Rogan even attended church services with his mistress. It got so that the pastor could count on Bailey and her pet always taking the same spot in the fourth pew on the right. And it amazed the clergyman to see the cat bow his head at appropriate times during the service, especially when a prayer was announced. Rogan seemed to love attending church services. Whenever Bailey took him for a walk, he would begin to strain at his leash, hoping to go into every church they passed. There was no question that the devout cat seemed happiest when he was healing people and when he was sitting in a church.

"With just a laying on of his paws, he actually cured a woman friend of mine who was suffering from chronic depression," Bailey recalled. "On another occasion, Rogan miraculously cured a clergyman's severe asthma."

Rogan did not have to be present to serve as the channel for healing energy. Once when the owner of a desperately ill Persian cat came to them for a healing, Bailey and Rogan went to church, bowed their heads together in prayer, and sent healing energy to the afflicted feline. In a few days, Bailey received a letter from the Persian cat's mistress saying that her pet was vastly improved and that the puzzled veterinarian, who had recommended that the cat be put to sleep, was "utterly awestruck."

Bailey recalled the time when a nearly hysterical woman approached her at a charity event, declaring that she could not take any more of life and wished to die.

Bailey suggested that the woman sit in the car with Rogan for a few minutes. The cat crawled onto the weeping woman's lap, then stood up on his hind legs, put his forepaws on her shoulders, and gazed into her eyes.

The woman said a great peace came over her. The headache that had seemed as though it might blind her suddenly disappeared—and the feeling of inevitable doom that had terrified her for months vanished forever.

Rogan lived to a ripe old age—but as every physical being must, he eventually moved on to a higher dimension of service. Jane Bailey, an energetic Englishwoman in her early fifties, continues to help people with their troubles and traumas through the agency of a four-year-old tomcat named Gus.

"I am convinced that Gus was sent to me by the spirit world to carry on in Rogan's pawsteps," she said.

As many as seventy seekers of healing per day come to the home of Bailey and Gus.

"These people pay nothing for their healings," she said. "Some of them feel better after merely stroking Gus. Sometimes he jumps onto patients' laps and gives them eye-to-eye contact. After a few minutes they leave feeling totally free of pain and anxiety."

In one press account, Canadian rheumatologist Dr. Raj

Patel was quoted as saying that he had referred five patients with degenerative knee joint disease to Gus. "And in each of these patients, the degree of severity was such that I truly believed that they were not amenable to correction. You can imagine my astonishment when three people—seemingly crippled for life—visited Gus and then almost danced into my office."

In Patel's assessment, to describe Gus the cat as a healer would be to "grossly understate his credentials."

In Bailey's cosmology, Gus is in contact with spirits, and he channels their otherworldly energy to help people and animals who are sick and need his loving services.

Would You Believe Flying Felines?

Back in 1959 there was all kinds of excitement about a flying cat in Pinesville, Virginia, and the ruckus over the bizarre beastie spread across the United States.

It seemed that Thomas—who was really a female but who had been named before that fact was discovered—had developed a true biological rarity: she had wings. And for ten cents, you could line up and see this wonder of nature for yourself.

Fifteen-year-old Douglas Shelton, who captured the winged feline while hunting in the hills, had nearly shot the critter before he identified her as a cat.

After Shelton had shinnied up a tree and caught her, he discovered that the animal had two bizarre lumps growing out of her back. On closer examination, Shelton saw that they were wings. When he touched them, the cat got mad and started clawing at him.

Other than a decided touchiness about her wings, Thomas had pretty good manners, and she seemed right at home with the Shelton family. Word spread fast about Doug Shelton's winged cat, and it wasn't long before a reporter from the Beckley, West Virginia, _Post-Herald_ came to examine the oddity with a journalistic eye.

For her many eager readers, Fern Miniacs described Thomas—whom she quickly identified as female—as looking very much like a large Persian cat with long, beautiful hair. The wings were furry and soft, Miniacs noted, but had a feeling of grittiness near the body.

"It's thirty inches long," Miniacs wrote, "has a tail like a squirrel, and two perfectly shaped wings, one on each side. The wings are boneless but evidently have gristles in them. Each wing is nine inches long."

A veterinarian who journeyed all the way from Baltimore to identify the growths on Thomas's back confessed, after a rigorous examination, that he had no idea how to explain the unusual biological occurrence of a cat with wings.

Thomas even had her day on NBC television's _Today Show_. On June 8, 1959, Doug Shelton told Jack Lescoulie, who was filling in for the regular host, Dave Garroway, that he had been offered as much as $400 for the incredible cat, but he was not tempted to sell her.

At the height of Thomas's national notoriety, a quiet, unassuming widow named Mrs. Charles Hicks, who lived on the Pinesville-Baileysville road, stepped forward and announced that the cat belonged to her.

The soft-spoken, gray-haired woman insisted that she did not wish to make any trouble for Douglas Shelton or anyone. She just wanted her cat back.

When reporters came to get her side of the story, Hicks

told them that the cat that Douglas called Thomas, she had christened Mitzi. A friend had bought the cat in California and had made her a present of the winged feline. All of her neighbors, she insisted, had become used to the sight of Mitzi and her wings, and every one of them could substantiate her story.

"One day I put some medicine drops in Mitzi's ears," she told the journalists. "Mitzi didn't like that and she ran away. That Shelton boy found her four days later."

When Doug Shelton refused to acknowledge Hicks's claim, she sued him for the return of Thomas/Mitzi.

On October 5, 1959, Shelton appeared in circuit court with a large Persian cat under one arm and a cardboard box under the other. The first thing everyone in the courtroom noticed was that the cat he carried most certainly had no wings of any description.

In embarrassed tones, young Shelton told the judge that Thomas had "shed" her wings in July. With a dramatic flourish, he opened the cardboard box and revealed two large clumps of fur.

"There they are, Your Honor," he said. "There are Thomas's wings."

Hicks indignantly proclaimed that the large Persian cat Doug Shelton had brought into the courtroom was not her Mitzi.

Ignoring the woman's protests and accusations, the judge awarded her one dollar in damages "for her trouble," and gave Doug Shelton custody of what now appeared to be an ordinary Persian cat.

The maelstrom of publicity over Thomas the Winged Cat quieted as quickly as it had begun. Doug Shelton and the big Persian cat disappeared into obscurity, and whether or not—as Hicks had suggested—the *real* winged cat flapped her bizarre appendages solely for the edification of Doug and his friends, the two of them never made it into the news again.

In his fascinating book *Strange Creatures from Time and Space*, John A. Keel recounts the tale of Thomas and Doug Shelton and goes on to detail an account of a large black feline with ostensibly functional wings that was said to terrorize Alfred, Ontario, in June 1966.

On Friday, June 24, Jean J. Revers, a confectioner, was startled by a creature he described as "looking like a big black cat—but with hairy wings on its back."

Revers told authorities that he had observed the astonishing flying feline swooping down on a neighbor's ordinary earth-bound cat.

The winged cat had "screamed like hell" as it tried to get away, Revers said. It took "gliding jumps of fifty or sixty feet—wings extended—after a good running start." He insisted the creature would remain a foot or so above the ground.

Revers fired five bullets into the howling, fluttering feline freak as it attempted to attack his neighbor's cat.

Police Constable Terence Argall told investigators he could not believe his eyes when he examined the thing Revers had killed: "It's head resembled a cat's, but a pair of needle-sharp fangs five-eighths of an inch long protruded from the mouth. It had cat's whiskers, tail, and ears, and its eyes were dark, greenish, and glassy. I never saw anything like it before in my life."

Further examination revealed that the flying feline had a wingspread of fourteen inches. Its pelt was sleek and black, and it weighed about ten pounds.

According to dispatches from United Press International, another flying cat was shot near Lachute, a village north of Montreal.

During 1966, at least three large black flying cats were reported in villages in Ontario and Quebec. Did someone forget to close the back door of the Twilight Zone?

Kiki, the Deva-Shan of Waikiki Beach

When is a cat not a cat? When it is a Deva-shan, a nature spirit, an elemental being disguised as a cat.

For fourteen very interesting years, Dr. Patricia-Rochelle Diegel and her husband, Jon-Terrance, lived with their beloved Waikiki Beau, also known as the Deva-shan of Waikiki Beach.

"You see what has happened in Honolulu as the high-rises and the condos keep going up is that the elemental spirits, the nature spirits, the Devas are being pushed out of their natural habitat in the South Pacific Polynesian jungles," Dr. Diegel said. "Consequently, in order to continue with their evolution, some of them must assume the bodies of certain animals, such as a horse, a cat, or a dalmatian dog.

"Why are those animals preferred? It seems to be because they all get kidney stones," she said, "though I don't know exactly what that has to do with it. Something about moving them higher up the evolutionary ladder."

Jon-Terrance, a bishop in the Antioch Catholic church, added that he had been told that the elementals would now begin to seek the bodies of domesticated animals, which were more highly evolved than jungle creatures.

The Diegels first made the acquaintance of Kiki when two of their students brought him to a class in metaphysics that the couple were teaching in their bookstore in Honolulu.

"They had found this small black kitten with golden eyes wandering in the Ala Moana shopping center," Patricia Diegel said. "They felt the cat was very special, so they just could not leave him to wander the streets. Neither of them lived in apartment buildings that would allow pets, so they didn't know what to do with the stray cat that they had felt was so unique."

But Kiki knew that he had found *his* humans. He jumped up on Patricia's lap, curled up on her shoulder, and slept peacefully there while she taught her evening class.

"At that time," Jon recalled, "Kiki was so small that he could fit in the palm of my hand. We stopped on the way home to pick up some milk and a can of tuna. Later that night, he slept on a pillow between us, a position he would maintain throughout his life with us."

Immediately the Diegels noticed certain peculiar things about the cat that they had christened Waikiki Beau. He did not meow; he did not like to play the usual "kitty-type" games; and he did not bother the bird cages Jon kept on the balcony of their ninth-floor apartment.

In her research, Patricia Diegel has observed that black animals are more highly evolved. "And highly evolved cats don't meow very much."

One night Patricia was awakened by Kiki, obviously trying to tell his mistress that something awful was afoot. She followed him to the balcony and there discovered that two stray cats had ascended to the ninth floor in hungry pursuit of Jon's caged birds.

"Kiki was not about to permit those stray cats to harm those birds," she said. "Those birds belonged to *him* and to Jon!"

Kiki also had the ability to pronounce certain words. Whenever he wished to be let out, he would approach one of the Diegels and say clearly, "Me . . . out!"

"Numerous guests distinctly heard Kiki accent the 't,'" Patricia said. "Kiki was not simply meowing to be let outside. He was saying, 'Me . . . out.' "

The Diegels also began to notice that Kiki had powers of precognition; he always knew which class members would not attend a session on a particular night.

"He would walk back and forth in front of the chairs assembled for class as if he were inspecting them; then he would jump up on the one particular chair of the student who for whatever reason would not attend that evening," Jon said. "And he was never wrong."

Kiki also had the ability to identify potential students who were heavy drug users.

"If someone who was into drugs would apply for class, Kiki would growl at them," Patricia said. "Since this came from a cat that almost never meowed or growled, we took immediate notice. Kiki would look above them and begin to growl as if he saw that they were bringing along negative entities in their aura."

When Sybil Leek, the internationally famous metaphysician and spokesperson for modern witchcraft, visited Honolulu, Patricia Diegel could not resist telling her about their Kiki.

"We were seated on the balcony overlooking the pool at the Sheraton when Sybil went into a light trance," Patricia said. "When she opened her eyes, she declared that our Kiki was really a Deva-shan, an elemental that had assumed the form of a cat in its evolutionary ascent. She pronounced him to be the 'Deva-shan of Waikiki Beach.' "

About this time, the Diegels acquired Fang Lei to keep Kiki company.

"I had always wanted a dog so that I could name it Fang," Jon said. "A dog just wouldn't work out with our lifestyle, so I gave the name to a cat. When people said Fang was an Oriental-type name, I added Lei to round out the nomenclature."

The Diegels noticed that Fang Lei was prone to getting lost or trapped—for example, inside a cupboard. Whenever his companion disappeared, Kiki would transmit telepathic images disclosing where they might locate Fang Lei and rescue her.

Some years later, when the Diegels were renting an apartment in Los Angeles downstairs from one of Patricia's old school chums, Kiki accomplished one of his most astounding astral projections and materializations.

"My friend Lois did not particularly care for cats," Patricia said, "so I would leave Kiki in our apartment with Jon whenever I came to visit her. On this one particular occasion, I glanced up from our conversation in Lois's apartment to see Kiki walking in the hallway from Lois's bedroom.

"As we both sat almost mesmerized, we watched Kiki walk into the room where we were talking, stand for a moment and look at me, then walk out of the room and *through* the screen door."

When Lois and Patricia went downstairs to the Diegels' apartment to investigate, they saw Kiki sleeping peacefully at Jon's feet.

"Kiki has been sleeping here for hours," Jon said when they told him they had seen the cat upstairs. "He hasn't moved a muscle—and he certainly hasn't moved from this room."

"Clearly," Patricia Diegel said, "Kiki had visited us in his astral body. When he walked across the floor in front of us, he looked just as solid as he could be. It was when he passed through the screen door that Lois and I knew that something was a bit strange about Kiki."

The Diegels could write a book about the paranormal experiences they shared with their beloved Kiki. The Deva-shan of Waikiki Beach left the physical plane when he was fourteen years old. Fang Lei lived to be sixteen.

"We have decided not to acquire any new cats," the Diegels told me as they prepared to move to Las Vegas in May 1992.

Jon's most recent favorite, Shaun, had just died, the victim of a bobcat attack in Sedona, Arizona.

"We love cats so much," Jon said, "but they leave such big holes when they die. We probably will never own another cat."

Although the Diegels have been my close friends for many years and they are truthful in all other respects, I knew this was a vow they would never be able to keep. As of this writing in November 1992, the Diegels own a "positively Aquarian" mother cat, Shangri-La, and her beautiful litter of four— Shamballa, Madame Pele, Shasta, and Indiana Jones.

We can only wonder how many of those cats are really elementals in disguise.

Establishing a Mind-to-Mind Link with Your Cat

There cannot be more than a few cat owners in the entire world who do not believe they have experienced at least one telepathic link with their pets. Comments such as "My cat always seems to know what I'm thinking," "I can call my cat just by thinking her name," and "I know he understands everything my husband and I say to him" are frequently heard whenever cat lovers get together.

I have already demonstrated the acute psychic awareness of cats in hauntings and other paranormal situations, and we

noted that cats are the familiars of witches in European tradition. Whether folklore or fact, cats are very often credited
with extensive extrasensory abilities.

Just as the vast majority of cat owners believe they communicate with their pets on some heightened level, a number of
real-life Dr. Doolittles claim that they communicate directly
with cats through their own ESP.

Ann Rubenson of Ellsworth, Maine, says she is a living
"psychic link" between people and their pets, and she consid-
ers it her responsibility to pass along various complaints animals may have regarding their living conditions.

Rubenson claims she has heard cats and dogs object to the
names their owners have given them and even to being given
hand-me-downs from previous pets. "I have nothing of my
own," one cat griped.

Samantha Khury of Manhattan Beach, California, lectures
on "The Secret Life of Pets," Urging her audiences to develop
a stronger mental and emotional bond with their animals.

"Close your eyes and picture your heart meeting your pet's
heart," Khury says. "Meet heart to heart, emotion to emotion.
Let them convey their feelings, thoughts, and the very essence
of their being."

If your cat should have a bad habit that annoys you, Khury
will instruct you to communicate with your pet through "mental imagery." Concentrate on the cat, think about its bad
habit. Picture in your mind the way you wish your cat to
behave. Visualize your cat doing what you want it to do.

Soon, Khury asserts, your cat will begin to pick up your
mental wish and obey you.

If your kitten is ignoring the litter box and using your new
Persian rug for her potty, Khury suggests that you "visualize
her running for the box and defecating into the litter. Picture

her urinating into the litter. Imagine the little sound it makes as it sprays. Get your cat's attention and tell her that you are thinking these things. She will understand that it is the right way to go potty."

Mystic Meg, a British psychic sensitive who writes a column on metaphysical matters for the *Globe* newspaper, shares her life with seven cats.

"Once a cat has established a firm mind-link with you, it can track you down anywhere," Meg says.

When Meg moved, she believed her cat Ruby would much prefer to remain at home with Meg's mother. Although Meg would be separated from Ruby by 300 miles, the cat had spent her entire fourteen years in the family home, and Meg was certain she would be more comfortable there.

However, the day after Meg left home, according to her mother, Ruby stepped out the door and disappeared.

Three months later, Ruby, no longer a chubby tabby, showed up, exhausted but happy on the doorstep of Meg's new home.

Meg said that as Ruby got older, she became deaf and blind. "One of the younger cats, Alice, became her playmate and guide," Meg said. "Alice could always predict when Ruby needed her, and it is this same sixth sense that cats use to warn humans of disasters."

Among Mystic Meg's advice on testing your own cat's psychic powers are the following tips:

While your cat is in another room, sit down quietly, and slowly tense and relax your muscles. Breathe in and out slowly for a minute. Close your eyes and picture your cat coming to you. If you have a true mind-link with your pet, he or she will soon be there.

Hide a cat treat somewhere in a room. Bring your cat in and picture in your mind where the treat is hidden. Give the cat thirty seconds to find it.

In the September/October 1992 issue of *Body, Mind, Spirit* magazine, Barbara Rosen quotes animal communicator Penelope Smith as stating that your attitude toward animals more than anything else influences how willing they will be to communicate with you and how easily you will be able to "hear" them.

"Many of us grew up believing that animals were 'inferior' to us," Smith said. "So we tend to talk down to them: 'Here I am up here with a big human brain, and down there you are with a little brain. What can you send up to me?' "

Animal communicator Carol Gurney of Agoura, California, expressed her opinion that "most animals like telepathy," but some may be shy, "and others are very private and feel 'It's none of your business.' And sometimes animals are just not in the mood to talk."

Gurney's advice to those cat lovers who really wish to tune into their pets' thoughts is to learn to still the mind. "If you have an endless stream of chatter going on inside your head, the animals will get a 'busy signal' when they try to reach you."

A Two-Minute Exercise to Still the Mind and Prepare You Mentally to Communicate with Your Cat

Many spiritual teachers speak of harnessing the energy of the Oneness of All Life to quiet the mind and to prepare for a more complete expression of unity with all life forms. Here is a simple exercise to help quiet the consciousness and bring about a greater awareness of the flow of communication between you and your pet.

Relax very deeply in the privacy of your room. Take three

comfortably deep breaths, hold each for the count of five before exhaling. With each breath you take, feel yourself becoming more and more relaxed.

Envision a brilliant light that surrounds your head, enveloping your body. Visualize the light moving all around you, bringing you peace, bringing you tranquility of mind, bringing you a quieting of all disruptive thoughts.

You know that the light has come from the very heart of the universe. You know that it is the light of goodness that emanates from the oneness that links all living things on the spirit level. You know that it is the light of unconditional love.

Visualize that light moving into you. Visualize the light of oneness actually becoming a part of you. Visualize yourself becoming at one with the light of oneness.

Know and understand that you must love and respect the sovereignty of all life forms.

Know and understand that when your mind is quiet, when all disruptive thoughts are stilled, you have the ability to communicate mind-to-mind with your beloved cat.

Know and understand that you have the ability to link hearts and minds with your cat in the energy of the Oneness of All Life.

Surround Your Cat with the Golden Energy of Love and Achieve a More Complete Mind-to-Mind Link

Here is a method that has been recommended by several psychic sensitives as a simple technique to help you achieve a more complete mind-link with your cat.

Sit quietly for a few moments in an attitude of quiet meditation and attune yourself to the Blessed Oneness of All Life. Whenever you spend a few moments this way, you are helping to undo the restricting attitudes of separateness between your-

self and the cosmos and are permitting the energy of oneness
to flow more easily through you.

Rise to your feet and know that you are going to demonstrate physically and audibly your ability to join the seen and
the unseen. Stand with your arms stretched forward, your
palms upward, and intone the universal sound "Om" in a
long, drawn-out flow—*Ommmmmmmm.*

Repeat the "Om" until you feel tingling in the palms of
your hands—until the skin actually picks up auditory
vibrations.

Then begin to project another type of energy toward your
palms. Begin to project the life force to your palms.

Visualize the life force passing through your fingers, moving
out to the palms of your hands. Focus on this until you begin
to feel a tingling sensation—almost as if electrical vibrations
are moving through you.

Next, begin to feel an actual, palpable force moving out of
your palms. Visualize a golden ball of energy hovering just
beyond your palms. Know that this is an energy of love, which
you are able to project to others.

Visualize that golden ball moving through the walls to en-
velop your cat companion, which you are picturing in your
mind.

Visualize your golden globe of love surrounding your beloved cat companion. See the love flowing from the internal
energy source, moving out from your palms, manifesting in
the golden globe, then transmitting thoughts of love to your
cat.

Now, in this connection of love, open your mind to receive
any energy which your cat is transmitting to you.

Once you feel you have completed a mental link with your
cat, you can intensify your communications and begin to develop any agenda you wish. You may conduct experiments in
telepathy at this point, or you may simply permit the oneness
to manifest between you in the energy of unconditional love.

8

FIND YOUR IDEAL CAT IN THE STARS

"I believe that it is nearly as important to know your cat's sun sign as it is to know the zodiacal position of your future husband or wife," one prominent astrologer told me not long ago. "Look at it this way: The relationship that you will have with your cat will be very intimate, conducted in close quarters over a long period of time, and you must learn to trust and to respect each other."

According to another successful astrologer with a celebrity clientele, the question of compatibility should be of primary concern when anyone decides on a feline companion. "By understanding the various character traits associated with the different zodiacal signs, you can better determine if you and the cat are going to get along."

Practitioners of astrology maintain that our individual personality is determined by the pattern of the heavens at the time of our birth—as well as our reactions, with relation to this pattern, to the stimuli of our environment during growth and maturity.

Although I am by no means an astrologer, I have many close friends who are; they have slowly convinced me over the years that there is *something* to be gained from the ancient lore of the stars.

I am most comfortable with those interpreters of the zodiac who claim that astrology is a science only inasmuch as mathematical plottings are used in the mapping out of horoscope charts. The rest of the astrological process constitutes an art, not a science—an art that provides its devotees with certain insights which may guide them around rough spots in life.

In numerous conversations with professional astrologers, I have been assured that competent interpreters of horoscopes are capable not only of predicting certain trends in their clients' lives, but also of revealing a great deal about character, personality, and temperament. Often, I have been told, a good astrologer needs only the knowledge of the sun sign under which the client was born to produce such information. Astrologers have also assured me that horoscopes can be cast for countries, corporations, or cats with the same precognitive accuracy that can be achieved for individual clients.

The following exploration of the zodiacal signs is offered only in the interest of providing you with another possible tool to use in building a successful relationship between you and your feline companion. The information regarding the various sun signs has been compiled from numerous conversations with successful and competent astrologers, but it is presented without claims of infallibility. You must, of course, know the birthdate of the cat in question.

Your own inner sense about your potential relationship with the cat you are thinking of acquiring—not someone's interpretation of the stars—should be the single most important determining factor. In the words of my dear friend the late John Pendragon, a remarkable astrologer and clairvoyant from Tunbridge Wells, England, "Astrology can be a very good servant, but an unreliable master."

The Aries Cat—March 21 to April 20

The Aries cat would prefer to rule the roost, so understand at once if you are considering obtaining a cat born under this sun sign that you may have to squelch the animal's desire to dominate.

The Aries cat generally has a strong resistance to disease, and is usually very robust. At the same time, this cat may be prone to accidents which affect the head.

If the Aries cat should succumb to illness, he or she will be inclined to run high temperatures, quite likely necessitating a visit to the veterinarian.

The Aries cat prefers rugged terrain. If you live in the mountains or in hilly country, your Aries pet will be in his or her glory. If you are a city-dweller, give your Aries cat a treat from time to time by taking him or her along on rides in the country. Just be certain that the air is brisk and keen if you should allow your Aries cat to wander, for this cat will rapidly become enervated in fetid, marshy terrain.

If you, the owner, should also happen to be an Aries, it will not be long before the fur will fly between you and your Aries cat. If you already possess an Aries cat, you have no doubt already noticed a great deal of strife between you and your feline companion.

Those born under the sign of Taurus will have somewhat more patience with an Aries cat than will an Aries owner,

but the Gemini cat lover would probably become quite annoyed with an Aries feline, as would an Aquarius, Virgo, or
Scorpio owner.

If you were born under the sign of Cancer, you would be
very unwise to take in an Aries cat. As a child of Cancer,
you thrive on quiet affection and gentleness, and you will not
receive such treatment from your Aries cat. If your sign is
Libra, you will discover your temperament is in decided conflict with an Aries cat. The same holds true if you are a
Capricorn.

A Leo owner and an Aries cat make the best match. Although a Leo also likes to be in charge, he or she will not
feel threatened by the aggressiveness of the Aries feline. If
you are a Sagittarian, you stand the next best chance of getting along with an Aries cat. A Piscean's tolerant nature
might also be able to adjust to the vagaries of the Aries feline.

The Taurus Cat—April 21 to May 21

Although the Taurus cat likes to have his or her own way,
this cat is not as demanding as felines born under the sign
of Aries. Taurean females make splendid mothers, extremely
attentive to their litters.

Taurus cats have a tendency to put on a little too much weight, and they will be a little less judicious about overeating than other felines in the Zodiac.

Your Taurean will also love being cuddled and coddled. Taurean cats are essentially love bugs, but they can become angry if provoked. Once they lose their tempers, they can become ferocious.

Taurus cats are susceptible to throat troubles, and there is also a tendency for their glands to be upset every now and

The Taurean cat will probably be happiest with an owner who is an accommodating Virgo. A Capricorn or a Leo could also enjoy a cat born under the sign of Taurus, but a Libran would be taking a bit of a gamble in acquiring a Taurean feline.

then.

Your Taurean feline will thrive best in an undulating countryside, well away from large bodies of water. An agricultural area suits the Taurus cat very well. Keep him or her away from industrial areas. Your Taurean seems to draw energy from the woods and large expanses of plant life.

If you, the owner, happen to have been born under the sign of Aries, you will not have a particularly good relationship with a Taurus cat. You are likely to find a great deal of fault with the Taurean feline, and the cat will cringe under your dictatorship.

If you are a Taurean, you will probably become impatient with your pet as he or she becomes older. You will be likely to be more affectionate with the cat in kittenhood. Potential owners under the signs of Gemini, Cancer, Scorpio, Sagittarius, Aquarius, and Pisces are also liable to become annoyed with the mannerisms of the Taurus cat.

The Gemini Cat—May 22 to June 21

You may have your hands full with a Gemini cat. This cat will quite likely to be very intelligent, but will also express a great deal of nervous energy—which can become very taxing. If you are an on-the-go sort, you will probably cherish your cat's seemingly inexhaustible energy.

That nervous energy, however, is likely to remain with your Gemini cat from kittenhood to maturity. You will also have to be aware that your cat is susceptible to lung problems. And like the Taurean cat, your Gemini pet may tend to overeat.

The Gemini cat functions best with plenty of room to romp. You will also observe that unlike other cats, your Gemini will seem to gain vigor from the wind and rain. Life on the Plains would suit the Gemini cat admirably.

A Gemini cat will get along very well with a Gemini owner; they will keep pace with one another. An owner whose sun sign is an Aquarius would also be compatible with a Gemini cat. Another possible combination would be the Gemini cat with the Aries owner.

A Libra, Cancer, or Capricorn owner would probably enjoy the Gemini cat for a time, but the cat may soon get on the owner's nerves. The same would probably be true of a Piscean or Taurean owner. A Scorpio owner would be well advised not to attempt a union with a Gemini cat.

If your sign is Virgo or Sagittarius, the possibility of harmony with a Gemini cat exists; but the happiest union probably lies between a Leo owner and a Gemini feline.

The Cancer Cat—June 22 to July 22

If you want a cat that will prove to be a great homebody, you can seldom do better than acquiring a feline born under the sign of Cancer. The Cancer cat may seem somewhat lethargic; it will exhibit little of the nervousness and restlessness displayed by certain other felines. You may notice, however, a slight fluctuation of your cat's mood during the full moon.

The Cancer cat has a generally cheery disposition; you may even notice that the cat shuns any gloomy or grouchy family member or visitor.

Your Cancer cat may come down with the occasional cold, and in his or her mature years will probably suffer from rheumatism. If you should wish to breed your female Cancer cat, have a veterinarian check her generative organs and womb carefully.

Although you won't find your Cancer cat enjoying a swim in a lake or the ocean, felines born under this sign do seem to have a certain affinity for water. A Cancer cat would love a home on the coast, or near a marsh or a swamp.

The Cancer cat will respond well to an owner born under the Taurus. There is also a chance of a good relationship with a Cancer or Sagittarius owner—if the human being does not tend to be overly critical.

If you are an Aquarian or a child of Capricorn, you would be well advised not to acquire a cat born under the sign of Cancer. Likewise, if your sign is Libra, Scorpio, Gemini, or Aries, you would be better off with a feline from some other zodiacal home.

A person born under Pisces is the perfect owner for the Cancer cat; in such a relationship the two-legged and the four-legged animal will walk almost as one. If willing to make a commitment to work at it, a Leo or a Virgo could also have a harmonious relationship with the Cancer cat.

The Leo Cat—July 23 to August 23

If you want to take prizes at cat shows, see that all your felines were born under the sign of Leo. Your Leo cat will love the limelight. Should entering contests not appeal to you, you will have a furry show-off at home.

Your Leo cat will exhibit a great deal of personal magnetism and will undoubtedly charm every member of your family.

Basically of robust health, the Leo cat may tend to injure the muscles of his or her back.

Adaptability is another of the Leo cat's most positive attributes; a Leo cat will fit comfortably into nearly any environment. If possible, you should see that it always has plenty of room in which to exercise. If your Leo cat could speak, it would probably express a preference for the mountains, rather than a swamp or a marsh, but it will provide you with excellent company wherever you choose to reside.

Since Leo cats are so adaptable, they are compatible with

most human beings. Their relationships will probably be stronger with those born under the signs of Aries, Leo, and Libra, and less satisfactory with owners born under Taurus, Scorpio, Capricorn, and Sagittarius.

Owners whose signs are Gemini, Cancer, Virgo, Aquarius, or Pisces will have to work a bit harder to make a solid union with the Leo cat, but the potential for harmony is there.

The Virgo Cat—August 23 to September 22

Cats born under this sun sign tend to be somewhat aloof. Cat lovers who adore their pets for being independent and self-contained should only acquire Virgo cats.

Although Virgo cats are usually not very strong physically, they are often quite long-lived.

In spite of their cool dispositions, they are extremely sensitive to discord. If there should be an argument in your family, you will quite likely have a cat with an upset stomach on your hands. Because of their tendency to digestive disorders, you will be advised to keep a careful check on your Virgo cat's diet.

Virgo cats fit in well on farms, in wooded uplands, and in areas where there are meadows and grazing lands. Keep your Virgo feline away from excessively damp places.

Taurean owners often get along quite well with Virgo cats. There can also be great compatibility with human beings born under Capricorn. Less often, positive relationships exist between Virgo cats and owners born under the sign of Aries,

Cancer, Sagittarius or Aquarius; these unions can be made to work if the owner is willing to exercise patience.

If you are a Piscean or a Scorpio, forget about acquiring a Virgo cat. You would be in for a bumpy ride almost fated to terminate in a collision. If your sign is Gemini, Leo, or Libra, don't acquire a Virgo cat unless you are also desirous of acquiring a nervous breakdown.

The Libra Cat—September 23 to October 23

If you have a comfortable bank account, go ahead and acquire a cat born under the sign of Libra. Libran cats love to be pampered and fussed over. They can make great show cats because they are especially proud of their appearance.

At the same time, your precious, pampered Libra pet will tend to be a bit on the moody and temperamental side.

The Libra cat tends to suffer from kidney problems, and you may expect bladder weakness as the cat grows older. In spite of these health troubles—and others that are more difficult to diagnose—the Libra cat generally lives to a ripe old age.

A house on a hillside would be heaven for the cat born under Libra. This cat would also be happy near the seashore, but you would have to monitor your pet's exploration of the cliffs and high rocky areas, for the Libra cat tends to be more attractive than graceful.

The Libra cat is unlikely to adapt to an owner born under

Aries or Capricorn. A compatible relationship can develop between the Libra feline and a human being born under Leo, Taurus, Pisces, Gemini, or Libra.

If you are about to acquire a Libra cat and you were born under the sign of Cancer, Scorpio, Virgo, or Sagittarius, think again. About the only sure thing for the Libra cat is a relationship with someone born under Aquarius.

The Scorpio Cat—October 24 to November 22

Once you gain the confidence of a Scorpio cat, you will have a passionate defender and a loyal feline—a cat that is very resourceful. Be prepared, however, for a flare of temper every now and again.

Scorpio cats can find it difficult to be kept in close quarters; they are happier out of doors and moving around the countryside. At the same time, their somewhat boisterous nature tends to make them a bit accident-prone.

As an attentive owner, you will have to keep a watchful eye on your Scorpio cat; this cat will often overdo if not kept under control. Should your Scorpio cat become ill, his or her temperature is likely to soar. Female Scorpio cats require special attention—especially if you should wish to breed them.

Basically, the Scorpio cat is very strong and will soon overcome nearly any illness. Your Scorpio is also blessed with great reserves of energy.

Scorpio cats can tolerate marshy ground and humid climates, but they are not quite as contented in cold, dry areas. Your Scorpio feline would be happy next to a large body of water or a large expanse of flat land, where he or she can roam every now and then.

If you were born under the sign of Aries, you should most certainly think twice before acquiring a Scorpio cat. You will eventually rub each other the wrong way.

Nor will the Scorpio cat likely be your cup of catnip if you are a Taurus, a Gemini, or an Aquarius.

You will be able to get along fairly well with your Scorpio fireball if you were born under the sun sign of Cancer, Leo, Virgo, Libra, Capricorn, or Scorpio. Owners born under Sagittarius or Pisces will be most satisfied with their Scorpio feline.

The Sagittarius Cat—November 22 to December 21

Your Sagittarius cat will probably drive you up the wall throughout his or her kittenhood; freedom and lack of restraint seem to be its main desires. With a seemingly endless supply of liveliness and fire, your Sagittarius cat may simply wear you out if you permit it to express the full range of its impulsive behavior. If the two of you can survive the wild days of your pet's youth, however, you will find that you have a good, solid friend.

You will also discover that even though your Sagittarius cat has mellowed a great deal with age, he or she has retained its vigor and attractiveness.

The Sagittarius cat has very few health problems, but you will need to look out for accidents to your pet's legs during his or her youth.

You can live nearly anywhere you please with your adaptable Sagittarius—as long as you make an occasional change of scene for your pet.

If you were born under sign of Gemini or Virgo, you have the least likely chance of complete harmony with the Sagittarius cat.

Owners born under Aries, Leo, Libra, or Aquarius will have the best opportunity for compatibility.

Be prepared for a bit more of gamble if you are a Taurus, Cancer, Capricorn, Sagittarius, or Pisces.

The Capricorn Cat—December 22 to January 20

Your Capricorn cat is likely to be somewhat on the moody side, and you will need to be especially kind and gentle to stay on your pet's good side. Under the best of circumstances, don't expect your Capricorn feline to be very demonstrative.

Interestingly, you will find that your Capricorn cat is more responsive to children or teenagers in your household than to any adult. You will also soon observe that your pet enjoys listening to music and watching certain television programs.

The Capricorn cat has a tendency toward rather poor health in kittenhood, and you may have quite a time settling on a proper diet for this cat's sensitive stomach. The Capricorn cat does become stronger with age, however; still, watch for rheumatism in the mature Capricorn cat.

Large cities do not appeal much to the Capricorn cat's moody nature, but this cat seems very much at home in rural areas. Capricorn cats make excellent farm cats and will do their utmost to keep the rodent population to a reasonable number. A dry atmosphere agrees better with the Capricorn cat than a humid one.

An owner born under the sign of Taurus has the temperament to create a very happy union with a Capricorn cat. A Virgo owner can also make a great match for the Capricorn cat.

There is some chance of harmony between a Scorpio owner and a Capricorn cat, and a Pisces owner could also make the relationship work.

A Gemini owner would have to learn to develop great patience should a Capricorn cat join the household, and Capricorn human beings should carefully consider the risk in acquiring Capricorn cats.

Be warned if you were born under the sign of Aries, Leo, Aquarius, Sagittarius, Cancer, or Libra: You are almost certain to consider a Capricorn cat in your household disruptive.

The Aquarius Cat—January 21 to February 19

The Aquarius cat is often moody and eccentric, but nearly always the model of feline independence. If you wish to keep this cat reasonably contented, take him or her along with you on automobile trips whenever possible; the Aquarius cat needs frequent changes of scene.

If you, the owner, are somewhat unconventional yourself, you will probably get along famously with the Aquarius cat. If you are basically a mellow person who doesn't sweat the details or allow yourself to become unglued over minor irritations, you will most likely have a tranquil Aquarian cat. However, if you are easily upset or tend to feel rattled and tense, you will quickly see your stressed-out Aquarian cat mimicking your behaviour.

Because of its tendency toward moodiness, the Aquarius cat flourishes best in an environment as free of mental and emotional tension as possible. And since he or she is sensitive to human stress, the Aquarius cat is also susceptible to digestive disorders.

The Aquarius cat likes to live where it is high and breezy. This cat will be uncomfortable near marshy country or stagnant water.

An Aries, Leo, or Virgo owner can establish a comfortable relationship with an Aquarian cat provided the owner is willing to allow for the cat's moodiness.

The Aquarius cat would take a long time to adjust to the lifestyle of a Taurean owner; Cancer or Capricorn owners probably just wouldn't be able to make the grade.

Owners born under Gemini, Sagittarius, or Pisces would eventually be able to establish a harmonious household with an Aquarius cat.

You will have the best luck with an Aquarius cat if you are an Aquarian or a Libran. If you happen to be a Scorpio, you would be better off seeking a feline companion from some other sign in the zodiac.

The Pisces Cat—February 20 to March 20

The Pisces cat is a very affectionate feline, usually blessed with high intelligence, but this cat does not possess great stamina.

Perhaps a bit too sensitive, the Pisces cat is very susceptible to illness and is usually not very strong. If this cat should live in a home where there is undue domestic strife, he or she will soon be on the road, seeking out a quieter domicile. Likewise, if there should be a gang of noisy children in the household, the Pisces feline will make himself or herself scarce in short order.

A serene environment would seem to be at the very top of the Pisces cat's requirements for happy living, and this cat will not thrive in a large city. The Piscean cat will most appreciate a place where there is water and an opportunity to stroll in the deep silence of nature.

There can be harmonious union between the Pisces cat and an owner born under Taurus, Gemini, Pisces, or Libra.

If an effort is made to work for harmony, a Leo or Scorpio owner can build a good relationship with a Pisces cat.

If you were born under Aries, Capricorn, Aquarius, Sagittarius, or Virgo, you would be better off not acquiring a Pisces cat. Both you and the cat would likely regret it.

However, if you were born under Cancer, you could enjoy a relationship with a Pisces cat that would far exceed your expectations. In fact, if your feline is a female, you might breed her in the hope of acquiring even more Pisces cats.

A Visit from the Ultimate Feline/Feminine Archetype

Imagine this: In one moment of linear time, you are standing in your farm home in Iowa, speaking with your older son. Suddenly you feel strange. You feel a bit queasy—and the next moment your face is scraping painfully against harsh grains of sand as you fall headlong onto the floor of an area in some faraway dimension of time and space.

That is what happened to me on the night I met Sekhmet, the lion-headed goddess, the ultimate feline archetypal expression of femininity.

I lay dazed and stunned on my face, and all around me I could hear what sounded like multitudes of hostile voices shouting for my death.

My god! Had I been transported back in time? Was I a fallen gladiator hearing the crowds screaming for my victorious opponent to administer the death blow?

I felt beaten, as though I could not move a muscle in my defense.

Then I slowly became aware of another chorus of voices that seemed to be on my side. They were shouting at me to get up. "You can do it," they cheered. "Put your legs under you. Breathe deeply. Live! Live!"

For the first time I was able to lift my head, and I saw what appeared to be an ancient arena for trial by combat. But in spite of the raucous calls for my death and the earnest shouts for my return to the fray, I could see no one.

Dimly I was aware that a figure stood near my fallen body. As I looked up to see whether it was friend or foe, I beheld a form that was unmistakably that of a woman with ebony flesh, but whose face was that of a dark-visaged lioness.

She reached down, took my hand in hers, and began to lift me to my feet. When she opened her mouth to speak my name and command me to get up, violent bolts of electricity shook my entire being.

Then the arena was gone . . . the black lion-headed woman was gone . . . and I was on my way to the hospital.

While I was struggling for my life in some in-between universe, my son and my wife had called an ambulance, fearing the worst after my sudden collapse.

I was released from the hospital the next day, after a series of physical tests turned up nothing. I knew all the examinations were unnecessary, but how could I explain to the doctors at the hospital that I had been taken to another dimension and saved from defeat in the arena by a black lion-headed goddess?

I knew that something very significant had happened to me on the night of December 2, 1974, at approximately two A.M., but it took me a while to determine exactly what—and, of course, I may never know the full meaning of my mystical experience.

I was barely home from the hospital when a close friend called to say that he had had a terrible dream in which I had been severely beaten, then rescued by a large, dark figure.

Another friend, a medium in Chicago, telephoned that evening to say that on the night of my out-of-body experience, she had had a vision in which she had seen me taken aboard a UFO to pass a test for a "higher plane initiation."

A few days later, a group of friends in San Francisco called to say that on the night of December 2, the lion-headed entity of Sekhmet had appeared to them as they sat in a meditative reverie. Sekhmet had transmitted my name to them.

Sekhmet, the lion-headed goddess, is one of the most ancient of deities, who came into Egypt in a time unrecorded from a place unknown. She is known as the Lady of the Place of the Beginning of Time and One Who Was Before the Gods Were.

A goddess of enormous power, Sekhmet defends against all forces of evil. She is also known as the Lady of the Flame; the solar disk depicted on her head in various Egyptian statues signifies her control of the sun. A consort of her husband-brother, Ptah, the creative process, Sekhmet is the one found most beautiful by Art itself.

Perhaps no other Egyptian deity was represented by so many statues, but Sekhmet was possessed of a dual nature. She was the goddess of both love and war, healing and pestilence, cursing and blessing. Magicians and priests who sought power knew that the greatest source of all lay in Sekhmet, but they were also aware that they must maintain a proper spiritual balance or they would provoke her ferocious wrath.

At that time, our family owned four cats: three large, smoky grays and one calico. I admired our cats' feline stateliness when they struck poses underneath the statue of the Egyptian god Bast that sat atop a bookcase, but I had no obsession with Egypt or with any cat god or any lion-headed deity. The statue of Bast had been a gift from my students when I had taught high school and had only sentimental significance.

The bizarre thing was that Sekhmet had seemed so real. I pondered whether I had journeyed to her world in a time outside of time or whether she had temporarily manifested in my dimension of time and space to present me with some kind of teaching vision.

At that time I was in regular correspondence with Robert Masters and his dynamic wife, Jean Houston, who had established the Foundation for Mind Research in Pomona, New York. When I was rummaging through some research papers Bob had sent me, I was startled to see that he had conducted a series of experiments in which he and a female subject had entered the archetypal symbol system of the Egyptian goddess Sekhmet and her "world."

As soon as possible, I traveled to the Foundation for Mind Research, where I was able to speak with Bob Masters, Jean Houston, and Michele Carrier, the subject in the Sekhmet experiments.

Masters explained a phenomenon in ancient Egypt called *Hanu*, which means "being seized by the god." And Sekhmet, through a statue of the goddess which Masters kept in a room, was regularly reaching out and grabbing people in the best ancient Egyptian tradition.

Michele Carrier saw Sekhmet as a historical representation of the archetype of the feminine. "Sekhmet exists within the collective unconscious," she said. "She comes from a primitive state in the evolution of consciousness, but the symbols that are there can evolve within the consciousness of someone today. They may be primitive symbols, but they're still active today."

Jean Houston expressed her opinion that Sekhmet's world existed in the archetypal imagination. "She is an avatar of the female warrior goddess. Sekhmet is an activating archetype in a particular Egyptian mode.

"I think that there is emerging in our time the rise of the feminine in the psyche. This energy is manifesting as the traditional goddesses who have contained a great deal of energy with regard to the activating anima, such as Isis or Sekhmet or Mary."

And what of the in-between universe or dimension in which archetypes such as Sekhmet exist?

Houston replied that she believed we are in a symbiotic process with it and that it has an "apartness" from us. "Reality is very thick," she said. "It is immensely complex."

Houston went on to express her pleasure and agreement with an image William James used in pragmatism. "We are like dogs and cats who inhabit our drawing rooms. You know, happy and thinking about the food and the nap and going bye-bye, but having no idea at all of the intricate and fascinating goings-on around the house or what's in the bookcases.

"I think that is our level of reality," Houston said. "We have a very, very tiny notion of what is reality. We are cats and dogs in the library. We are a psychospiritual process of which our own coding has barely been tapped."

According to Houston, such images as Sekhmet and other figures that may be considered deities or holy personages by certain individuals are able to become a reality to those who experience their manifestation. "And it isn't just a reality that dwells inside," she said. "It has an objective reality."

Such an image as that of Sekhmet relates to older areas of the brain, and thus is more related to the autonomic system, she explained. "An image may impart a wave form to the bioplasmic field around. That wave forms to other kinds of frequencies, which then begin to attract what is necessary or even create that which is necessary.

"So can thought become flesh or attract its own objective reality through the impartment of the wave fields? Yes!" Houston said. "And that will be a way to explain, in part, the appearance of Jesus or the Virgin Mary or Sekhmet. Any image that is held long enough and intensely enough tends to become incarnate—incorporated and corporeal in the symbiotic environment."

Find Your Cat's Power Animal in the Native American Zodiac

When I was describing my extraordinary experience with the archetype of the goddess Sekhmet to my friend Sun Bear, the great Chippewa medicine priest, I pointed out how strange it seemed that I should have an encounter with an Egyptian entity. Anyone who knows me or my work is aware of my great attraction to American Indian medicine power. It would seem, therefore, that my vision might have been more likely to manifest itself saturated with Native American symbology.

"But Brother Brad," Sun Bear said, smiling. "We are always saying that all is one. Now you must also believe it. You see, you are born under the sign of the Cougar, so it wouldn't be strange for an entity that would appear as a great cat to come to your rescue in the in-between universe."

I was puzzled. Sun Bear knew I had been adopted into the Wolf Clan of the Seneca nation by the Repositor of Seneca Wisdom, Twylah Nitsch. What did he mean by saying I was born under the sign of the Cougar, the Mountain Lion, the Puma?

"Yes." He nodded. "The wolf may be one of your totems, but the great cat is your medicine wheel symbol."

That was when Sun Bear explained to me about the medicine wheel cosmology that he had realized through his visions and had expressed with the assistance of his medicine helper, Wabun. The Great Mystery had revealed to him a Native American zodiac, complete with representative totem animals.

I am certain that many readers respond to the colorful and dynamic symbols of American Indian medicine and would like to know how to determine their cat's (and maybe their own) totem power animal. Simply find the birthday of your cat below and study the implications for a better relationship between you and your feline companion. Some people have given their cats stuffed animals representing their totem animal or placed drawings of their feline's totem animal above the pet's bed in order to increase the pet's opportunity for better balance on the Earth Mother. Remember, to the Native Americans all life is one—and your cat is entitled to a power symbol just as much as you are.

The Red Hawk—March 19 to April 19

Those born under the Native American zodiacal sign of the Red Hawk are likely to be adventurous and assertive. They cherish a desire to be free, and those closest to them may sometimes consider them a bit headstrong.

The Beaver—April 20 to May 20

Those of the Beaver sign are generally blessed with good health. They cherish peace and security, and they are thought by all to be loyal and stable.

The Deer—May 21 to June 21

Clever and talented entities are found under the sign of the Deer. Your Deer cat will exhibit a generally positive disposition and will sometimes appear to be a creature of perpetual motion.

The Brown Flicker—June 22 to July 21

Entities born under this sign have a strong nesting instinct and are usually deemed to be good parents. Brown Flicker beings love peace and quiet and seek to avoid serious conflicts.

The Sturgeon—July 22 to August 21

Sturgeon beings have a great ability to teach others. They may be considered a bit domineering, but they generally bring a positive approach to every problem.

The Bear—August 22 to September 22

Entities born under this sign of the Native American zodiac are usually slow, cautious, and quiet. Your cat companion born under the sign of the Bear is probably a no-nonsense feline that seems to be able to detect insincerity in others.

The Raven—September 23 to October 22

Raven beings are sociable and energetic, full of nervous energy and fluctuating moods. They are generally very flexible and adapt well to new environments and circumstances.

The Snake—October 23 to November 21

Charismatic but often difficult to comprehend, Snake entities often present a problem to those around them. Beings born under the sign of the Snake may hide a deceptive nature behind a charming exterior.

The Elk—November 22 to December 21

Elk beings are competitive and athletic, but they are also patient and kind. Entities born under the sign of the Elk enjoy a change of scene every now and then—and cherish a strong independent streak.

The Snow Goose—December 22 to January 20

If your cat companion was born under the sign of the Snow Goose, you have a feline that is content to stay at your side and that generally shows little interest in any dramatic alterations of the daily routine. Far from sluggish, however, the creature born under the sign of the Snow Goose has great stamina.

The Otter—January 20 to February 18

Otter beings are often regarded as unpredictable and mercurial. If your cat was born under the sign of the Otter, you will have a feline companion that will generally be good-natured and a loyal friend.

The Cougar—February 19 to March 20

Cougar beings are mystical. You will probably experience some fascinating telepathic link with your Cougar cat. Watch your tone of voice and your nonverbal communication as well, for those born under this sign are very sensitive and easily hurt by disapproval or rejection.

0-452-27095-2 . . . . .

 Plume

STRANGER THAN FICTION

(0452)

☐ **BEYOND NEWS OF THE WEIRD by Chuck Shepherd, John J. Kohut and Roland Sweet.** News Junkies of the world, rejoice! Gathered here in one hilarious volume are more than 500 of the weirdest, craziest, most outlandish true stories ever to find their way into our nation's newspapers.
(267161—$8.00)

☐ **MORE NEWS OF THE WEIRD by Chuck Shepherd, John J. Kohut and Roland Sweet.** Just when you thought it was safe to read the Sunday papers comes this volume with over 500 of the most bizarre, the most shocking, the most unbalanced stories—you won't believe your eyes. (265452—$8.00)

☐ **NEWS OF THE WEIRD by Chuck Shepherd, John J. Kohut and Roland Sweet.** Just when you thought you'd already heard it all, here comes this hilarious volume with over 500 strange-but-true stories that proves once and for all that facts are far weirder than fiction. (263115—$9.00)

Prices slightly higher in Canada.

Buy them at your local bookstore or use this convenient coupon for ordering.

PENGUIN USA
P.O. Box 999, Dept. #17109
Bergenfield, New Jersey 07621

Please send me the books I have checked above.
I am enclosing $_____ (please add $2.00 to cover postage and handling).
Send check or money order (no cash or C.O.D.'s) or charge by Mastercard or VISA (with a $15.00 minimum). Prices and numbers are subject to change without notice.

Card # _____ Exp. Date _____
Signature _____
Name _____
Address _____
City _____ State _____ Zip Code _____

For faster service when ordering by credit card call **1-800-253-6476**

Allow a minimum of 4-6 weeks for delivery. This offer is subject to change without notice

There's an epidemic with 27 million victims. And no visible symptoms.

It's an epidemic of people who can't read.

Believe it *or* not, 27 million Americans are functionally illiterate, about one adult in five.

The solution to this problem is you... when you join the fight against illiteracy. So call the Coalition for Literacy at toll-free **1-800-228-8813** and volunteer.

Volunteer Against Illiteracy. The only degree you need is a degree of caring.

FP14

0-452-27095-2 . . . . .

 Plume

COMIC RELIEF

☐ **IF CATS COULD TALK by P.C. Vey.** Here are 90 hilarious cartoons concentrating on our furry little feline friends and just what they might be thinking and saying about people. It's more fun than a ball of yarn.   (266424—$6.00)

☐ **EXCUSES, EXCUSES by Leigh W. Rutledge.** A witty, enormously entertaining compendium of Rationalizations, Alibis, Denials, Extenuating Circumstances, and Outright Lies.   (269210—$6.00)

☐ **COUNTDOWN TO THE MILLENIUM compiled by John J. Kohut and Roland Sweet.** Hilarious-but-true news dispatches heralding the end of the planet.   (269156—$8.00)

Prices slightly higher in Canada.